# KNOWLEDGE B
## THA LADY FIERCE SAGA

*Hood Square Series – Book 3*

Other Books by Knowledge B

Hood Square Series:
Tha Khronicles
Tha System

For permission requests, contact: Hood Square, LLC
ahworks12@gmail.com
facebook.com/kbtooreal
facebook.com/hoodsquare
instagram.com/@tharealhoodsquare
Visit our Web site at tharealhoodsquare.com

Printed in the United States of America

First Edition: 2023 Library of Congress Cataloging-in-Publication Data Works, Abdul-Hakim Tha Lady Fierce Saga / Knowledge B--- 1st ed.

ISBN: 979-8-35090-917-3
ISBN: 979-8-35090-918-0

1. African American---Fiction. 2. Drug dealers---Fiction. 3. New York, New York---Fiction. 4. Phoenix, Arizona---Fiction. 5. Washington, DC---Fiction. 6. Maryland---Fiction. I. Title.

# ACKNOWLEDGEMENTS

First off, I would like to say al hamdu Allah (all praise be to Allah) for blessing me with the talent to turn my thoughts into written words. As I continue to publish my own novels, I continue to see my admiration grow for my favorite authors whose books gave me some much needed company while I refused to sit idle and bored inside a prison cell. My mind continues to fly free as an eagle in open skies!

I want to take a moment to give a heartfelt shout out to my beautiful big sister Latoya Gentry and my beautiful grandma Ms. Etta Mae Doss. I love and miss them more than I can express. RIP big sis. RIP grandma. I continue to make du'a that Allah have mercy on both of my cherished love ones' souls!

I give a wholeheartedly shout out to my beautiful parents: Billy and Twilla Works. Dad, more than ever I continue to look up to you and respect the man you have always been. I don't know any more stand up and solid than you. Mom, I continue to love and cherish you. You will always be my twin. I'm proud to get my good looks from you beautiful. Thank the both of you for literally loving me and supporting me for every second of my life even before it officially started!

To my little brother DeAndre "Outlaw" Works. I know times been a little harder with first losing Grandma and then big sis who always had our backs even her sickly years. Nonetheless, I tell you to continue to keep your head up and best believe your big bro got you. In'sha Allah (God willing), one day we will be reunited on the other side of these prison gates. I hope you enjoy my latest book like you did with *"Tha Khronicles"* and *"Tha System"*. I love you lil bro!

To my big bro Eugene " Lil Gene" Gentry. Just like I said with lil bro, I know life has been a lot different without big sis in it, but we continue to honor her by living our lives with purpose and doing something with them. I love you big bro and thank you for being there for big sis. I find solace that she had one of her brothers with her until the end!

To my beautiful big sister Trina Marquez. I cherish you more than ever and will always put in the extra effort to stay in touch with you to let you know your baby bro do care about you. I love you and hope you and your kids are doing well!

To all my beautiful nieces and handsome nephews, I hope I continue to lead by example and inspire y'all that dreams can be caught no matter your situation in life. Just dare to chase them!

To the rest of my extended like my beautiful cousins Tahnisa "Big T" Edwards and Tyaneisha "Ty" Moody. I love y'all more than y'all really know. Our bond has been more like one of siblings. To my big relative Dewayne "Frankie J" Johnson. To y'all kids, my baby cousins, I hope seeing me continue moving forward in life shows y'all that not even being captive in a prison cell can stop somebody who wants more out of life. Dare to live life to the fullest!

To my relative Darius " Dee Ru" Agboghidi. I love you relly. We are getting closer to finally walking out of these prison gates in'sha Allah. We have been on this main line getting close to twenty solid years now. Keep your head up family!

To my young author-in-training Just Jaylin. I want to give you another extra special shout out for helping like you did with *Tha System,* by helping me get my final edits together for this book. You keep striving and writing because one day the world is going to see just how amazing of a writer you are once you start to publish your own works of fiction in'sha Allah.

To my homie Vincent Parker aka Vince P. Thank you Sida for being a true friend and coming through in the clutch to help me get this book to the world. I will always be grateful. Prominent Music forever!

I want to give a special thank you to my pen sis, the very talented authoress Pyper Chanel for all your insight into DC and its unique lingo. Aye young lol!

With that said, I can't forget my home girl M. A. Vazquez from the Bronx. Thank you for helping me with crucial info about your hometown. Boogie Down lol!

To all my fellow incarcerated people. I continue to push hard and hope I can be an inspiration to all of you that you can truly impact the type of change needed in y'all lives to change the narrative. I'm proud to be an incarcerated author, entrepreneur, brand ambassador, and mentor. In'sha Allah, one day I plan to be out and coming back into this broken system to do my part as a volunteer to assist as many as possible to transition back into society. Until then, I want you all to look up and keep it locked like that with ten toes standing firm!

To my hardworking team at BookBaby who continue to put in countless hours to make my books available to the world at large because from a prison cell, I'm now global. Thank you all!

I thank all my fellow Hood Squares for buying my books and being invested in the brand because it's not a moment, it's a Movement! Yours Truly, Knowledge B aka Tha Real Hood Square!

"*Success is not measured by the position one has obtained, success is measured by the obstacles one has had to overcome to succeed.*"

—**Outlaw** *aka* **DeAndre Works**
*2020 Browning Unit aka SMU Two*

# SAGA ONE:

# Sasha

# CHAPTER ONE

## 1993

The last thirteen months had been rough for twenty-five year old Sammy Garcia aka Genuine. He had been forced to sit and languish on the infamous Rikers Island as a result of some bogus gun charge two of New York's finest had put on him in an failed attempt to get him sent back upstate for the long haul. Nonetheless, his very expensive Jewish mouthpiece had finally figured out a way to get everything tossed out once he had dug up some dirt on one of the arresting officers who happen to have a bad gambling habit. It was money will spent.

Now he was back on the mean streets of the Bronx, New York where he had learned the rules needed to survive any situation that life had threw at him. He was happy to be back with his wife Sabrina who had unfortunately had to give birth last year on August twenty-first to their firstborn without his presence due to him being away. Genuine couldn't find the words to describe the joy and love he felt to get to be around his wife and son who they had named Santiago after her deceased father. Both of their fathers had been friends way back in the Dominican Republic and had migrated to the United States together to pursue dreams of one day playing in the MLB, but had ended up making it all the way to the NYC where they originally settled in the Upper Manhattan neighborhood, Washington Heights before Genuine relocated to the Bronx as a runaway teenager.

Life outside never stop moving, so Genuine wasn't shocked to see that some things had changed in the time that he had been away. This was in fact the Big Apple, the city known to never sleep. The borough of Manhattan was just down the way from his stomping grounds. He and his manitos which was what they called each other in Spanish because they were really a band of brothers, were thinking about ways to take their hustle down there because Manhattan was really where the big money was at. They already had some clientele from there who were bold enough to come through and buy dope from the spots they controlled with an iron fist throughout the South Bronx. Some of his Kings had already migrated to parts of Harlem and were in the process of curving out territory for the nation to expand down that way.

The Bloodline had really exploded throughout the city since he had first become a member while doing a four year bid upstate back when he was just eighteen years of age. Prior to joining, Genuine had been a very unruly teen with no sense of purpose or direction in life. He had been a straight hoodlum who wasn't afraid to take what he felt was his by any means necessary, and had went to the extreme on multiple occasions to get it. This had led to him getting arrested for an arm robbery and for the first time in his life having to go do time. His first year in prison had been spent relatively like his life on the streets had been which was him being a brute who took advantage of anybody too scared to stand up to his madness.

Nevertheless, his bad behavior had finally came back to really bite him in the ass when he had mistakenly tried a member of the Bloods which outraged the entire organization on the yard. Consequently, the Bloodline being an organization that took care of its own which was opened to all of the Latin prisoners inside Tha System approached him with a proposition that he couldn't refuse, because the other option was to stand alone against the wraith of a very powerful prison gang that didn't mind getting brutal with its enemies. At the time, he may have seemed like a mindless savage, but he wasn't no dummy in the least because he immediately took the offer. Therefore, his life as King Genuine began. He was required for the first time in his life to really start instilling discipline and living in order instead of the chaos he had become so fond of in his teens as a street thug. He quickly learned the ways of Kingism and rose through the ranks. Genuine to his surprise was a natural born leader. All he ever needed was some guidance. His father, nevertheless, had tried many times before to get him to correct his behavior, but his old fashion Dominican ways just couldn't reach his new school hardcore American-born son.

In 1990, Genuine got out at twenty-two years old as a newly transformed man. This had led to him and his wife Sabrina, who had known each other most of their lives to become a couple after she had been impressed that Sammy the savage was no longer moving around like he had no care for life. She also got down with the Bloodline as a Queen and started to help him as he enforced order in the streets.

The Bronx was his chosen home and many people who had known him before his first bid especially those in his age group couldn't resist the appeal of Kingism that he and a few of his fellow Kings were preaching. As a result, they were able to quickly build up their ranks outside of prison where their organization had originally started. Amor De Rey was being felt by those who had grown up not really knowing love at all. For many of his manitos, this was their first time knowing what having a family felt like because it was mandatory for every member to be his brother's keeper. When one King moved, all Kings moved. Every member no matter what rank was to follow this principle which was why even Genuine as a high ranking member still got his knuckles bruised on the skulls of enemies who occasionally encroached on to their turf. This was to show his Kings that none of them would ever be allowed to grow soft and fat.

"Amor De Rey," said the group of Kings who had been waiting patiently in the apartment for Genuine to arrive which was located in the Mott Haven Housing Projects which was a stronghold of their ever expanding territory within the South Bronx.

"Amor De Rey," Genuine said as he stepped inside accompanied by his bodyguard and enforcer Mario who was a Chicano that had proven himself very loyal to the Bloodline after becoming one of the first to join the newly formed Bombers Tribe back when Genuine had gotten out of prison.

"Okay it's sure feels good to be back and see all my twins still standing strong and multiplying," Genuine said as he addressed his manitos doing a quick headcount to make sure that everybody was in attendance for this very important, highly secretive council meeting he had called for his tribe.

"And it sure feels good to have you back as well twin," Bronco said, who was Genuine's right hand man as his Cacique. Bronco was a six foot two Puerto Rican man who didn't mind busting a head or two just to get an understanding. They had originally met while doing time in prison and had become very close during their warrior years of putting in work for their nation. Once they had gotten out, Genuine hadn't hesitated to invite the Spanish Harlem native to come live in the Bronx and help him curve out territory.

"While away, I was getting reports that some of our rivals had been revving up their attempts to invade our territories all around the Bronx," Genuine said referring to the three murders of his beloved manitos that occurred in three separate occasions.

"Yes, we took a few hits over this last past year, but they didn't go unanswered," Blade replied who was a very short Puerto Rican man that had made a name for himself within the nation and throughout the Bronx as being a cutter because he couldn't be found without his two pocket knives and also kept a razor under his tongue most of the time. In the short amount of time he had been a member, he had shown himself to be very useful and willing to go on the missions that even the most hardened of Kings secretly cringed about.

"And that I know to be the truth, but the message hasn't been heard loud enough that when you mess with us we will destroy you," Genuine said looking every one of his maintops in the eye to let it sink all the way in that he was back at the head of their local chapter and he wasn't going to tolerate the blatant disrespect that these three murders represented.

"Amor De Rey," Genuine said as he put his right hand up and threw up the hand sign of the crown they would all kill to defend.

"Amor De Rey," the Kings all replied throwing up the exact same hand sign with their right hands.

The meeting was adjourned, and the message had been passed on to all the ranking members in his tribe that war had been declared. Therefore, they were going to squash their enemies like they always did which was through lethal precision like they had learned from their nation's fledgling years inside the Big House. They were without question, the most dominant gang in the Bronx, but that didn't stop their enemies who surrounded them from literally taking a shot at the throne. Since his awakening, Genuine was no longer a big fan of violence, but knew the dangerous world that they lived in required it if his tribe and nation were going to continue to be able to live long and prosper.

# CHAPTER TWO

The streets of South Bronx had gotten even more dangerous to be in as his tribe started to kick up the war with two of their most hated rivals, the BBGs short for the Body Bag Gang which was a large black gang that was a part the Bloods, and then there was the Los Arañas which was a small but deadly Puerto Rican gang primarily from the Mott Haven neighborhood. They had a fierce reputation for being widow makers. It had been three weeks since they had officially declared war on the both of them for the deaths of three Kings who had been beloved members of his tribe. Genuine had been outraged about each one as he had sat locked down inside Rikers Island. However, this time inside the jail had been totally different than his first experience with the island that set in the East River between the Bronx and Queens. As a high ranking member of the Bloodline, he had been well taken care of by the dozens upon dozens of Kings from all over the five boroughs who were doing time spread throughout the huge jail complex. His organization was now one of the most powerful in the state of New York and was spreading rapidly into the surrounding states. He was already hearing about Kings running things in places like New Jersey, Rhode Island, and Connecticut.

Nonetheless, his tribe and nation still needed to make money especially in times of war because war cost money. His soldiers needed to be well equipped and well feed to take on the burden of defending Amor De Rey. Genuine had plans to conquer more territory for his tribe as he set his sights on getting deeper into the lucrative drug trade inside his borough. This was in fact the Empire State, so he had to keep an empire state of mind as he operated.

"So what are the Columbians talking about now?" Genuine said as he watched six of his most trusted Queens breaking down the kilos of cocaine they had just received a day ago.

"Inca, they are saying that they can give us a way better deal than what we are getting from yo Dominican relatives," Bronco replied as he too surveyed their growing operation.

"You know I'm all for the better deal, but I don't like how them Columbians do business. We have heard how they come with mad strings attached twin," Genuine said referring to rumors he had heard from some of their fellow Kings out in Brooklyn.

"Yes, I know twin, but the prices make it worth our while. And we can use the increase in dope to help us gain more influence and more allies as we expand," Bronco said as he followed his closest homie and mentor back to the makeshift office they had set up in the basement where their secret stash spot was currently at.

"I'm going to have to really consider this because you know how I'm using our business dealings with my Dominican familia as an olive branch to broker a better relationship with them than we have had in the past. We have to continue to win the minds and hearts of more of our Latino brethren to show them that this Amor De Rey is real and is the only way for our people to survive the onslaught we are facing from all those opposed to the uplifting of us. United, we are a force to be reckoned with," Genuine said as Bronco nodded his head in agreement.

"You know I feel you because for far too long we have allowed these fucking Italians and Irish muthafuckas to think that they are the shot callers for the city. It's been our time to rise up and show these muthafuckas the might of our nation," Bronco said angrily which was his nature because he was known to be one of the most passionate in the tribe. This made him real good at his job as the Cacique for the Bombers Tribe aka the South Side Tribe because of their stronghold in the South Bronx. Genuine trusted Bronco to the fullest and while he had been away, it had been Bronco running things on his behalf and carrying out his orders with no hesitation. His tribe had continue to grow even in his absence which showed that they were really built to last. Even the upper management above him were impressed with both his leadership skills and the success of the spread of the Bloodline in the Bronx, especially in the Southern parts. His tribe was responsible for the entire borough and were also using their growing influence to establish their nation down in Spanish Harlem which wasn't that far away.

"Yes I do and you know we all share that same sentiment which is why we continue to push forward with our cause," Genuine said leaning back in one of the comfortable office chairs they had gotten from some boosters they knew from the East Bronx.

"We are also having success with getting our message out loud and clear in the streets that when you fuck with a King, you gone get crushed. Our soldiers have been very active and from what I hear, we have dropped two BBGs and one Araña to add to the body count we already had before you came home. But we have also almost took a lost with one of our peewees getting critically wounded the other day hanging with some of the other young Kings on a Hundred and Sixty-third Street by the Hunts Point," Bronco said.

"Yeah, I caught wind of that. Find out his name and tend to his and his family needs, so they know they have the full support of their tribe behind them. I want us prepared for a long drawn out war if it comes down to that, but I'm liking what I'm seeing and I'm foreseeing that it won't take months to get what we want," Genuine said as he signaled for his top enforcer to step inside.

"Inca Genuine, what's good?" Mario said as he immediately stepped into the small makeshift office. "I'm good twin. Listen, I want you to get with Blade and let him know that I want him as well as you to accompany me and Bronco to Brooklyn next week because we have got word from upstate that all the Incas for every tribe in the five boroughs and Jersey are to meet and discuss the political climate of the streets. I've been selected to head this meeting and report the details upstate to upper management," Genuine said dusting off the new black and gold Timberlands he had just got because he liked to stay sharply dressed even during his day-to-day operations. This was something all Kings prided themselves on, to never get caught looking like a bum because they were royalty which is why they wore black and gold as their official colors because these colors never got old.

"Amor De Rey," Genuine said.

"Amor De Rey," both said in unison making sure to give their Inca the proper respect.

Genuine was happy that progress was still being made. They still had a lot of obstacles to overcome, but things were going as good as they could given the circumstances they were dealt. During his time away, his tribe had secured reliable NYPD connections within the forty-first precinct that was starting to be worth all the kickbacks they were giving them on valuable information to keep the police off their asses and some on the movements of their enemies which had led to them robbing two stash spots their enemies thought were safe. Their contacts which were two old school narcotics detectives with a long history of busting balls gladly accepted their thirty percent finder's fee which came out to be over a quarter million dollars. This was way more than he had got as the head for his tribe, but he wasn't into taking from his tribe because he knew what that type of greed did to a family. He liked to show the Kings under him that he wasn't afraid to get his hands dirty at times and earn every dollar and notch he had on his belt. He had personally carried out a hit last year prior to the bogus arrest that got him sent away.

Nonetheless, he still had to be careful because he knew that the two crooked cops that had tried to screw him over still had some pull with their brethren within the force even though they had long since been transferred to other precincts since the controversy surrounding his arrest. This put a target on his back. Since getting out, Genuine had been very cautious in how he moved around because he was always looking over his shoulder for a tail. When he had to come to secret meetings or visit a spot like the one he was in, he would simply make sure to slip whoever may have been watching him through tactics he had learned from some of his Kings with military training. At the moment, he had their police connections checking if there were official or unofficial tails following him and from what he was hearing, there were no whispers within the department about seeking revenge on him in any way.

He, however, still wasn't taking any chances, so he had went as far as to keep the location of where he was officially staying a secret for fear of his family being targeted by one of his many enemies. Only his most trusted manitos like Bronco, Mario, and Blade knew where he was living when he did go home, two to maybe three days out of the week. The most important things in his life outside his nation were his wife and son. He had made his wife Sabrina to her displeasure fall back on her duties of running the tightknit group of Queens within their tribe who were very much equal members of the Bloodline, and in his opinion, way more lethal than their male counterparts. Their nation had a zero tolerance policy on any disrespect or abuse of any kind against its members which included every female who had proven herself worthy of becoming a Queen.

# CHAPTER THREE

---

The day of the big meeting had arrived, so Genuine along with his ranking officers were making their final preparations before they all left to make the trip down to Brooklyn. For the past week, he had been in constant communication with his fellow Incas and other top ranking Kings from most of the other tribes in the city and beyond to make sure they were all on one accord for safety and security reasons. The other day, he had been accompanied by Mario who as his main enforcer had become his bodyguard and the top security expert for his tribe to go scope out the location where the meeting was going to be held. The location as well as the meeting were all suppose to be top secret. This information was only given to the various Incas and their most trusted advisors, but he knew that something this size was hard to keep a tight lid on which made it even more important to be prepared for any situation where an enemy or the police decided to crash the party even though it would be considered suicidal to do so. This meeting was like the hood version of a United Nations meeting with world dignitaries.

He was dressed to impress as well as his entourage who all were rocking the royal colors of black and gold. They all had on their beaded necklaces which Genuine only required to be worn on special occasions like today in order to conceal the identity of who had rank within his tribe to avoid being high value targets by their enemies. Both he and Bronco wore beaded necklaces with a sequence of five black beads followed by two gold beads, but his necklace had a solid gold lion's head hanging from it. Mario and Blade both wore necklaces of solid black beads that represented the death they would bring to their enemies. He looked at his most trusted advisors who all possessed the power and grace needed to continue to rise up in their nation. He knew that in the event that something ever happened to him, that his tribe would be left in good hands to carry on.

Nevertheless, he was grooming Bronco to eventually run the small subtribe down in Spanish Harlem which for the time being would still fall under the banner of the Bombers Tribe in the Bronx even though he had been hearing rumors that Brooklyn was trying to claim Spanish Harlem as part of their tribe which he knew wasn't going to happen with them already being deeply connected with their Bronx brethren. Bronco had grown up in Harlem and had strong family and community ties out there. Genuine knew that Bronco was perfect for the position, and would some day become an Inca over his own tribe especially if the Kings population continued to grow within Harlem and throughout other parts of Upper Manhattan.

They were currently in the neighborhood known as Mott Haven where they had been gaining more control. It was the most southern part of the Bronx. Genuine had decided to use it as a base for his expansion operations into both Upper Manhattan and the Bronx. Their turf within the Mott Haven Housing Projects wasn't as unruly for them as some of their other spots like the Webster Housing Projects where they were heavily beefing with the BBGs over.

"Amor De Rey," Genuine yelled as he looked out into the assembly of his fellow Kings from all over the tristate area.

"Amor De Rey," they all shouted with their right hands raised high throwing up the crown.

Genuine took a moment to let the emotions that had stirred up calm down because he had came a very long way in the last seven years from that uneducated hotheaded street thug. Prior to becoming a King, he had had a speech impediment that made him stutter his words which made him consequently too embarrassed to express himself verbally growing up. This had led to him becoming very good at expressing his displeasure of being humiliated and picked on through fighting very hard which earned him the fear he had thrived on as a youth. Once he had joined the Bloodline in prison, he quickly had found out that he was required to sharpen all his skills which included to his dismay at first, his abilities to communicate and the art of persuasion. It had took him many hours of being tutored by his fellow incarcerated Kings before he started having the confidence to speak in front of others including crowds which had helped him ultimately rise up through the ranks in the manner he did because there was no upward momentum in their nation for being just a brute. He had learned that brains would always get him a lot further in life than brawns.

"As I look into the mirror, I see a beautiful reflection. It's such a joy to see all my twins, male and female living prosperous. However, our enemies are many and they will stop at nothing in their quest to destroy our almighty nation. We have gathered here today to insure that we are on one accord which is our way because when one King moves, we all move. Therefore, as we continue to grow, we have to stay true to the Kingism that got us here. Our enemies want to divide us up, so they can turn us against each other. This will never happen because the glue that bonds us together will never unstick. For many of us, this is our first encounter with each other, but as we embrace, we could tell that our souls have always known its brother and sister," Genuine said as he paused to survey the room full of faces. They had chosen a warehouse that was owned by one of the Kings from Brooklyn to meet up where they had space and didn't have to worry about any unwelcome interruptions. He remembered when he had first joined that they hadn't been no more than one hundred strong in the whole state with majority of them being incarcerated. Now they were everywhere and were never going away.

"Amor De Rey," Genuine yelled once again after he finished up his speech that had taking him almost thirty minutes to deliver because he had lived in the moment and allowed it to articulate his words in a way that had to have touched every heart in the room.

"Amor De Rey," they yelled even more passionate than when he had started.

The rest of the meeting was spent discussing a wide variety of topics concerning the future of their nation which included what was expected of them from upper management and giving aid to those tribes living in areas where their enemies were strong. Since his tribe was one of the strongest in the nation, he had committed them to helping out with two tribes in New Jersey. Genuine knew that upper management was going to be somewhat concerned about some of the things reported back to them, but overall things were moving forward.

# CHAPTER FOUR

Things had gotten even crazier out there in the streets ever since her tribe had declared war against two of their most hated enemies in the South Bronx. This and a few other things had led to her husband Genuine sending her and their one year old son Santiago way out to Pelham Manor in Westchester County north of the Bronx for safe-keeping. She completely understood his fears, but Sabrina Garcia was starting to go more than a little stir crazy sitting all cooped up for most of her days with nothing but a growing toddler to keep her company since her husband spent most of his time way in the Bronx overseeing the day-to-day operations of their tribe. He would only come home two, sometimes three days out of the week to spend time with his family. Consequently, she felt like he was still locked up on Rikers Island where they had gotten married because he feared that the bogus gun charge was going to stick and get him sent back upstate for a very long time. Fortunately for them, the lawyer that was known to represent clients who were big-time players in the New York underworld had somehow got his case dismissed.

Nonetheless, she was going to talk to her husband about moving back to the Bronx once things calmed down because she had her own responsibilities. In her own right at only twenty-three years old, Sabrina had become the top Queen in their tribe not based off her relationship with Genuine. She had shown on a few occasions just how down for the cause she was through defending their nation against rivals. One such incident involved her fighting along side her husband when she had first became a Queen when they had ran into a group of rivals while visiting one of their new spots that their tribe had acquired in the East Bronx. She hadn't hesitated at all to jump in with the brash knuckles that her husband had given her once the fighting started. It had been five of them which included her as the only female against eight rivals. The skirmish had came to a sudden end after Blade had badly slashed up two of their rivals which made the rest run for the safety of their turf, carrying their injured homies. The only injuries she had received that day was a busted lip from a lucky punch that had landed due to her momentarily becoming distracted by the screams of the first rival Blade had stabbed.

Growing up in Washington Heights with three older brothers had toughened her up because they had made sure that she knew how to properly defend herself. Therefore, for years she had trained as an amateur boxer and because of her looks, people tended to write her off as just another pretty girl who was too scared to chip a nail. She had learned to use this to her advantage because being underestimated gave her the opportunity to operate without being seen, and by the time they did notice her, it was most likely too late to stop her. These things had helped her gain the individual respect from the members of her tribe and had led to her fellow Queens looking up to her for guidance and leadership.

The only people who were allowed to come visit were her mother, brothers, and in-laws who did stop by to check on her, but their visits always seemed to end too quick. She found herself spending hours talking on the phone to her fellow Queens and some of her home girls she had came up with. They were always asking her where she was and when was she coming back which led to them poking fun at her that she had become some fugitive of the law. Sabrina loved them and so desperately wanted to be around her crazy group of friends. Most of them were always begging her to pull up to do their hair since she had built up a reputation for being one of the coldest hair stylist in the Bronx and probably in the whole city. This hustle did generate some good steady income that had helped her stay afloat while her husband had been away. Her thoughts were broken by the cry of her son, so she went back into the room that had become his nursery to check on him.

"My beautiful pretty-eyed baby boy," Sabrina cooed as she gently bounced him in her arms which seemed to always have an instant calming effect on him. She loved this growing bundle of joy and would do anything to protect him which was why she had stayed put for so long. Her son was the physical manifestation of the true love she shared with her husband. She had been proud to give him a son as his firstborn and had felt honored that he had decided to name their son after her long deceased father instead of making their son a junior like originally planned. The phone which was located in the dinning room started to ring as she was finishing up feeding Santiago.

"Hola papí," Sabrina said lovingly to her husband because she just knew it was him checking in.

"Hola mamacita. How are you and my hijo doing?" Genuine said feeling the emotions stir because he missed them dearly and couldn't wait to be with them again. It wasn't easy staying separated like this from them, but for the time being he knew it was for the best as he got things in order. Nonetheless, he knew that his wife wasn't feeling being so far away from the place that had raised both of them.

"Mi esposo, when are you coming home because I'm tired of being without you?" Sabrina said because she couldn't hold back how she was feeling now she was hearing his voice.

"Mi esposa, I will be coming back later tonight and I swear I will spend Thanksgiving and the next two days afterwards with you and my baby boy," Genuine said knowing that he had to be home in time to wake up to spend Thanksgiving with them. He knew that her mom and brothers were coming with their wives and kids. He was expecting his parents, one of his brothers that he always been close with, and his baby sister Marie who always idolized him to all come as well. The rest of his siblings were strongly opposed to him being a King and not a DDP short for Dominicans Don't Play like them which was based out of the Washington Heights, so they were forbidden to know where his family stayed. The DDP were rivals of his tribe which was why he never went to visit his old neighborhood now that he had become such a high ranking King for safety reasons because he knew that if the opportunity presented itself, he was too high valued of a target to pass up.

"Okay, because I was wondering if you was really going to be able to make it. This is going to be our first Thanksgiving as a married couple and we are the hosts this year by default," Sabrina said pausing for a second to let the reference to her current predicament sink in, "Because I knew you wasn't expecting me to continue fixing all this food by myself."

"Aww, I know mi amor. My mom has been on me about not spending enough time with my family. Mi esposa, you know that I'm not enjoying one second apart from y'all. Not in the least. I love you so much," Genuine said.

"And I love you too mi esposo. I know the life we live and the responsibilities that come with it. But that still doesn't make it any easier to be without you. But I don't want you feeling guilty in any way okay," Sabrina said.

"Okay mi amor. Just know the time is coming when I will feel comfortable having y'all back in the Bronx. I don't like living way in Pelham Manor also. It don't have that upbeat vibe we know and love in the Boogie Down Bronx," Genuine said as he went to beat boxing which made his wife, a bona fide lady MC like her favorite rapper MC Lyte immediately start to rap over the phone.

"Baby you already know," Sabrina said laughing after she went in for at least a minute straight off the top of her head because she was cold with the lyrical flow. They were true lovers of Hip Hop which was the same thing for all Bronx natives because their borough was the birthplace of it. She remembered growing up in the 'Eighties seeing all the breakdance crews and lyricists coming from all over the Bronx to battle each other. Those were the times to be around because they were a part of their culture and history. Hip Hop had really grew since then, and now in the 'Nineties, it could be found everywhere. The music and art coming out nowadays were as unique and diverse as its adherents.

# CHAPTER FIVE

It was looking like it was going to be a good Christmas for real because things were going better than expected. Genuine on the advice of his Cacique, had linked up with the tribe in Brooklyn and together they had brokered a better deal with the Columbians. Therefore, his tribe was now able to continue to expand their influence outside of the Bronx. They were using the network of tribes throughout the tristate area to supply their fellow Kings with the dope they were getting while also helping out their incarcerated Kings through a clever smuggling operation that gave their nation the resources it needed to continue to be a force to be reckoned with inside Rikers Island and the various correctional institutions throughout upstate New York.

The kickbacks he was receiving were really adding up and he had over two million dollars stashed at his home in Pelham Manor. He was already thinking about moving his family back to the Bronx since things had to died down with the war between his tribe and the BBGs who were the bigger threat due to how large and well organized they were. They had come to a temporary ceasefire over the turf battle inside the Webster Housing Projects which the BBGs considered as the heart of their territory because it was where they had originated. This had been accomplished through the influx of dope his tribe was now touching which made the BBGs come to the table in order to start buying work off them for a way better price than they had been getting elsewhere.

Nonetheless, they were still at war with the Los Arañas in Mott Haven who had started employing guerrilla style tactics against them since they were vastly outnumbered by his tribe. They had recently targeted two different dope houses his tribe was running in the neighborhood. In response, he was able to amp up security and so far these attacks weren't hindering their operation, but it still was an irritation like a splinter in an elephant's foot which could get infected if not properly addressed. Therefore on the advice of Blade, he had put out a terminate on sight order against an Araña who went by the name of Creeper. He was rumored to be the secret leader of the Los Arañas and the one personally responsible for pulling the trigger that led to the death of the King they had killed while Genuine had been locked up. The war with them had unfortunately resulted in losing two more from his tribe which made the current body count: three Kings to the five Arañas they had successfully knocked down. He had to start treating them like the group of venomous spiders they prided themselves to be and not get caught up in their deadly web of deception. His tribe had to operate like pest control and eliminate this threat before it became out of control.

It had really gotten cold since winter had started. The state had already been hit by two different Nor'easter storms. This, however, was a part of living life on the East Coast where the weather could be even more dangerous than their rivals lurking in the shadows. Genuine who had grew up in New York was prepared like any other native and had his winter gear all the way on point. This was in fact the time of year when native New Yorkers really put their sense of fashion on full display.

"Amor De Rey," the group of the Kings said immediately as they saw Genuine and other ranking members of their tribe walking through the grounds of the Mott Haven Housing Projects which was a complex comprised of eight large apartment buildings. The Bombers Tribe operated in five of the buildings with the other three being the home turf for the Mack Elevens which was a predominantly black gang who had allied themselves with the Kings earlier on. This small gang also aided the Kings in their war against the Los Arañas who was a hated rival for the Mack Elevens as well. The relationship between them had deepened even more once the Mack Elevens had started helping his tribe run dope into New Jersey.

"Amor De Rey," Genuine, Mario, and Blade all said in unison making sure to return the crown salute to their soldiers who were out doing various things to keep this part of their growing South Bronx kingdom moving forward. Genuine made sure that every member of his tribe no matter if they held rank or not knew that they were loved and respected by their Inca. He had been schooled very well while in prison by some of the Kings who were now a part of the upper management that ran their nation. They had shown him how to be a very effective leader through gaining the hearts of those under his management. He had been taught that every good leader was truly an even better follower of his people because it was his job to make sure his people's needs were well attended to in order for his rule to be able to continue on. The Kingism they believed in wholeheartedly was in place to help avoid the development of tyrants who breed rebellion which was in contrary to the cause of his nation. They were truly trying to uplift their community.

"So I want to make sure we have everything in order for the toy drive we will be running on Christmas Eve," Genuine said as he looked at his soldiers, "This year has been rough for everybody, so we want to brighten things up by showing some Christmas spirit through giving back. I loved what we did for the eve of Thanksgiving by giving out free turkeys to families in need. We are the protectors of our community. We are far from being the menace the media and mayor has tried to portray us as lately. I will be making sure everywhere we hold a strong presence continues to see what we truly are about. Our enemies hate us simply because we build up wherever we go and don't tear down like they do which exposes them for the frauds they are. Amor De Rey will forever be felt."

"Amor De Rey, Amor De Rey, Amor De Rey," every King and Queen in the courtyard and nearby went to chanting as they threw up the crown. It felt like the earth quaked right under their feet as if it could feel the King's Love penetrating all the way to its core.

Genuine looked at his soldiers with pride because seeing how far they had come never got old.

The only one missing out of his most trusted advisors was Bronco because he had finally been sent to his native Harlem to oversee the subtribe's operations. He had understood that his presence was needed there more than the new home he had fell in love with over the last few years because he was born to lead and had really came a long way like Genuine since their days on the yard smashing the skulls of anybody who dared to challenge the Bloodline. They had been warriors who had proven themselves on more than one occasion to be willing to put their lives on the line for the cause they loved with every fiber of their beings. He remembered two different riots they had been in where they had been the clear underdog in the brawl, but still had somehow came out on top. He had seen how much power they had had as a few and how their enemies inside had started to steer clear of further confrontations with the Kings. Now as many, they were truly an unstoppable force that was bringing a reckoning upon all those who opposed them.

He couldn't wait to surprise his wife by telling her that he wanted to have her and their son with him when they passed out the toys to some of the many underprivileged kids in the Mott Haven neighborhood. This was one thing that always touched his heart to see so many of his people living in poverty. This went for black, Latino, and Native people. As a Dominican, Genuine was a mixture of all of them. He never shied away from acknowledging both his African and Native roots because he was proud of them. This was the case for many from his tribe and nation who were mostly members made up of Puerto Rican descent, but they had a growing membership of his fellow Dominicans as well. Nonetheless, they all were mostly Latinos who derived from the Caribbean that had a deeply blended heritage of the various Native island tribes, Spanish settlers, and African slaves. This blend could be seen in both their distinguished cultures and features.

He decided to stay in the grounds with his soldiers because there was no safer place to be at the moment. It was suicide for any rival to make a play at him with so many of his loyal Kings around. Nevertheless, his top enforcer Mario was on high alert as usual. Genuine knew that his good friend wouldn't hesitate to give his life in service to his Inca. Mario was military trained from his days as a Marine which he had been passing on to the soldiers of their tribe to better equip them with the skills they had been using lately. He had been thinking about sending Mario temporarily to the West Bronx to help their tribe's efforts to gain a foothold there because they had been receiving some heavy resistance from the local sets out that way who so far had been successful in keeping his tribe out of their neighborhoods and projects.

# CHAPTER SIX

## 1994

The new year had officially came and passed. They had gone out with a few of their fellow Kings and Queens from their tribe to the world famous Times Square in Manhattan and braved the cold, crowded conditions to watch the ball drop that had sealed the old year forever. Time was the one thing constantly moving forward which signified that the world never stopped spinning, not even for a second. Sabrina had been happy though to get to spend some very romantic moments alone with her husband after they had ditched their entourage. They had left their son in the care of her mother who had been more than happy to come spend some quality time with her grandson.

She was happy that she would be moving back to the Bronx in the next few weeks after successfully pulling her husband's heart-strings because things had settled down a lot every since their tribe had secured an uneasy alliance with their former rivals, the BBGs. Sabrina knew that the allure of money and power could always change the minds and hearts of men because they all for the most part desired the same things. This was why the BBGs had made the smart choice to align themselves with the Kings to use the drugs they were getting in weight to grow their own organization which went all the way up Webster Avenue from their home turf in the Webster Housing Projects to parts of the East Bronx. Nonetheless, she couldn't deny that she hadn't grown some type of attachment to the serene living of Pelham Manor. The four bedroom house they had been renting was the most space she had ever lived in at once because she had grown up living in close quarter apartments that had at the most three bedrooms. However, since she had been the only girl and the youngest, she had been for the most part afforded her own room while her three older brothers all shared a room until one by one they had all started to move out. On the low she had secretly became a suburbanite who enjoyed going down to the market for fresh vegetables and fruit. Sabrina would never admit this to nobody not even her husband who was her best friend that his hardcore Queen had gotten a little soft over these past months.

Nightfall had already came in, so it was dark which meant most of her neighbors had settled in. This was in contrary to the areas she had been accustomed to living in where the freaks really did come out at night to party and find whatever fix they needed to make it just one more moment before they had to do it all over again and again. For the most part, her neighbors who were mostly white had welcomed her in with opened arms, but she kept them at bay because they had gotten into a habit early on of asking too many questions about why her husband stayed gone a lot. She just couldn't deal with nosey neighbors snooping all in her business for no other reason at all than being a bunch of bored housewives.

She had just finished putting her son in his crib after feeding him and bathing him. He was her precious baby boy. She was so in love with her little twin who had inherited his pretty colored eyes from his father's side because he had the hazel eyes that his paternal grandfather had who just couldn't get enough of bragging about it to whoever would sit there and listen. She didn't mind his stories though because he would also tell her tales about her own father and their days back in the Dominican Republic to how they had migrated to the United States landing in Florida before finally making it to their final destination in the NYC. Her in-laws were a very vibrant bunch who kept her entertained every time they were over. Her personal favorite was her little sister-in-law Marie who like her father could talk up a storm. She had turned nine years old last month in December and couldn't stop telling everybody that she was no longer a little girl, so she didn't want them treating her like a baby. All Sabrina could do was shake her head in agreement because she knew once Marie set her mind on something there was no telling her otherwise. Plus, she remembered how she used to be when she was around that age of being both the youngest and only girl in the bunch. This was why they were so close and really shared a sisterly bond between them.

Walking back into the kitchen, Sabrina could of swore she heard a floorboard creak which immediately alarmed her because she had no visitors. However, this was an old house, so she let her nerves settled back down as she went to make her a simple turkey sandwich with cheddar cheese, sliced dell pickles, lettuce, and tomatoes on top because she had restocked at the local deli earlier. The rye bread was her favorite to make these types of sandwiches with because of its grainy texture.

As she walked back into the living room to settle in and see what was on TV while she ate, she was suddenly confronted by an intruder wearing a masked holding a straight razor. She could see the smirk through his mask. Nevertheless, she couldn't panic because she had to keep him away from her son which made her feel dread at the prospect of his intentions if she failed to stop him.

"You already know what time it is you fucking puta," the masked intruder said menacingly as he took a step towards her.

"Please, please, I am married. You can have whatever of value there is in the house. Just please don't do this," Sabrina pleaded playing the role of defenseless little housewife he clearly had put her in.

"I came for you puta. You are the one valuable. I'm going to have fun with you before I kill you. I hope yo fucking husband dies slowly on the inside after he views yo mutilated body because I fucking hate y'all. Y'all have some fucking nerve calling y'all selves Latin Kings and Queens like that gives y'all the right to take whatever the fuck y'all want. Creeper sends his regards puta," the masked intruder said right before he lunged at her.

As a result, Sabrina's instincts and years of training instantly kicked into overdrive as she smashed the porcelain plate right into his face and followed with the glass of water she had in her left hand. He immediately stumbled, but quickly recovered. Now outraged, he wildly swung the straight razor at her. She barely had time to get out of the way as she ran in nothing but a robe with some house slippers on back in the direction of the kitchen to grab a knife or something to use as a weapon to defend herself. The intruder was close on her heels and was trying to get a hold of the back of her robe for leverage, but she made it far enough to grab a cast iron skillet she had thankfully neglected to put away. Not wasting a second, she turned on her heels and without a moment to spare, swung the skillet with all of her might, consequently, connecting on the left side of his face. This made him crumble immediately as he fall face first into the floor. The next few moments were a complete blur as she blacked out with rage from the audacity of him to attack her in her own home with her son not that far away. She just kept on hitting him and hitting him in the back of his head until a bloody mess was everywhere including all over her.

Sabrina finally came to after sensing that he was no longer a threat. She could tell by the lack of movement and how much blood was spilled that he was dead. Now she went into panic mode because she didn't know what to do, so she immediately paged her husband to get him to call. Therefore, a little over a hour later he along with Mario, Blade, and a few others from their tribe pulled up. She was still in the kitchen watching him to make sure that he wasn't playing possum with her because she feared what he would do to her son if she let him get the best of her. Nonetheless, she hadn't noticed that her son had been crying for the last twenty minutes.

"Mi amor, it's okay I'm here. Baby, I'm here," Genuine said as he immediately rushed to his wife's side and went to holding her tight.

"Mi esposo, mi esposo," Sabrina mumbled as she went to shivering and crying on his shoulder.

His enforcers quickly cleared the whole house and the backyard to make sure that there was no more surprises. Mario came into the living room carrying a now sleeping Santiago to show his boss that their son was okay. Genuine ordered them to make preparations to clean the mess up and throw the scum into the East River in multiple pieces. He was outraged and wished he could bring the piece of shit back to life to kill him again and again himself. He picked his wife up and carried her to their bedroom to clean her up and get ready to take her and their son to a safe house in the Bronx. He couldn't believe that somebody had made a play for his family in their secret home, but he was going to make everyone involved pay with their souls.

# CHAPTER SEVEN

The war between the Bombers Tribe and Los Arañas had gotten bloodier since the failed hit on his family. As a result, the streets of South Bronx were even more treacherous to be in especially inside the Mott Haven neighborhood where both his tribe and Los Arañas claimed as their strongholds. The Los Arañas operated not that far away out of the Mill Brooke Housing Projects which was also located inside Mott Haven. His tribe so far hadn't had any success in gaining any ground inside their projects. It was a guaranteed death sentence for any King or Mack Eleven to get caught slipping over there.

Genuine still couldn't believe that they had somehow found out the secret location of his home in Pelham Manor. He had thought that he had took all the necessary precautions to avoid having any of his enemies ever get the drop on his sanctuary. Now he had his family close with him inside the Mott Haven Housing Projects where his tribe had put the lockdown on the building where he was staying to make sure that the only people allowed entry were residents and approved members of his tribe. He was currently living in an apartment on the top floor where Mario had multiple soldiers spaced out in the hallway to keep close watch on anything suspicious which would be met with deadly force.

It had been a month since the incident in Pelham Manor and the heat was still turning up. In the weeks following the incident, his tribe had successfully knocked down five Arañas, but had lost three more soldiers because more enemies who's hatred for the Kings seemed everlasting had took the opportunity to start trying to stop the advancement of his tribe inside their turfs.

To make matters worse was the fact that he had just found out that his wife was pregnant which made it even more essential to keep her safe and secured where he could see her daily. Sabrina, however, was very strong, perhaps the strongest person he knew. His Queen was the fiercest, most beautiful woman that he had ever met. She wanted Creeper's head on a stick for what had he tried to do to them, so Genuine had promised his wife that they were going to get their revenge soon enough. Nonetheless, the leader of the Los Arañas had become like a ghost in the streets because nobody could pinpoint his whereabouts. Genuine had even put a sizeable bounty on his head in hopes to get somebody inside his organization to bite, but the Los Arañas were very disciplined and loyal to their leader. He secretly respected their tenacity which made them worthy adversaries. This would only make Creeper's death even sweeter because Genuine knew that his rival would slip up eventually, and when that happened, he planned to be the one dealing the death blow.

Nevertheless, it was business as usual because Genuine still had obligations to fulfill. His nation was working extra hard to distribute the dope they were getting each week to all their customers, wholesale and street corner alike. They had developed a network that spread throughout the five boroughs of NYC and was slowly going down the Eastern Seaboard. He knew the dope they were getting was now hitting the streets of Washington, DC. The Nation's Capital had proven to be a very profitable market with a growing appetite for the quality they were getting from the Bloodline.

"Amor De Rey," Genuine said to his closest homie as they embraced.

"Amor De Rey," Bronco replied as he went in for a bear hug.

"Okay, okay, I've missed you too. I must admit it," Genuine said laughing because it did feel good to be around Bronco who had really came into his own since taking head of their subtribe in Harlem. He had successfully helped the Kings expand throughout Harlem and in small parts of Upper Manhattan. Consequently, there were serious talks about acknowledging them as their own tribe which would immediately put Bronco on top of the list to become the newest Inca inside their nation. Genuine was really pleased to see his manito doing good. They had been keeping in touch over these last few months mostly through talking over payphones to avoid potentially having their conversations recorded.

"Yes, it's always good to look in the mirror and see my reflection looking back at me handsomely. I missed being in yo presence twin," Bronco said as they sit down inside Genuine's apartment.

"Likewise twin. Even though we both know yo good looks from me," Genuine said jokingly.

"I take no shame in that because it's a honor to have been under yo tutelage twin," Bronco said seriously with a smile.

"We have learned so much from each other twin. This relationship of ours is mutual. So how have things been out in Harlem?" Genuine said knowing already a lot from the reports he been receiving directly from Bronco, but he wanted to hear the latest.

"Well you already know that we have expanded into other parts of Upper Manhattan and are also working on solidifying our turf inside Spanish Harlem. We have been able to gain more influence through converting smaller Latin gangs to our Kingism and then being able to put them to work with the dope we have been getting from the Columbians," Bronco said.

"Okay, I'm glad about the progress, but what's going on with the trouble you've been having with them muthafuckas from Harlem Crip," Genuine said.

"Yeah, these muthafucka'n Crips are starting to become an annoyance twin. We been beefing with them tough over turf because they jealous of the influence we been having inside what they consider to be their hood. We have already lost two Kings to the bloodshed," Bronco said angrily.

"You know if needed, I can have Blade gladly come assist you with this because he has been having success helping the tribe finally gain some ground in the West Bronx," Genuine said.

"Nah, because he needs to keep his focus on the mission at hand. Plus, we still have these muthafucka'n Arañas to exterminate out here. I'm still pissed them pack of spiders had the nerve to crawl into the home of my Inca. If you didn't order me to stay in my post, I would have came back on a killing spree twin. But we will handle Harlem Crip like any other enemy we have faced, with no mercy until they bow to our rule or become extinct," Bronco said passionately.

"I know you would have came without question, but like you said about Blade, you have to keep yo focus on the mission at hand. And Harlem and the rest of Upper Manhattan are yours because yes, you are going to be running yo own tribe. They are going to need their Inca putting all his attention on the continued growth of his tribe. I'm going to call in a vote in the next meeting because it's time. Brooklyn feels the same way," Genuine said fully acknowledging that the subtribe should become the newest tribe in their nation.

"I'm honored you feel this way twin. I've known that this was yo plan from the beginning which is why you sent me back to Harlem in the first place. I ain't gone lie, it sure feels good to be in my old stomping grounds. Mi familia is happy too to have me around a lot more," Bronco said emotionally.

"What are you two big softies talking bout?" Sabrina said as she came into the living room which made both quickly rise from their seats. She quickly kissed her husband and hugged her manito who couldn't help but hug her like the bear he was.

"It's sure is good to see you my Queen. Sammy told me that you was sleeping peacefully with my nephew, so we didn't want to disturb y'all," Bronco said as he let go of her.

"Francisco, you know that y'all should have came and let me know my brother-in-arms was here for a rare visit nowadays. I've been hearing how our newest Inca been handling business in Harlem," Sabrina said taking a sit on the arm of the recliner her husband was sitting in.

"I know manita, but I wouldn't have left without saying good-bye to you and my nephew. I can't wait to see just how big he has gotten since the last time I seen him," Bronco said smiling thinking how she was one of the only people who could get on him and his Inca without fear. It could be said that she was the real leader of their tribe because they all listened to her words and would all die in service for her. It was clear that his manito really loved and respected his wife which was a prime example for the rest of the tribe on how to properly treat their Queens.

They spent the rest of conversation catching up on family matters. Bronco couldn't stop offering congratulations once they let him know about Sabrina's pregnancy which they had been keeping a secret between them. They still hadn't shared the news with their parents or family. Genuine wanted to keep a tight lid on this for awhile until they couldn't hide it once his wife started to show for safety purposes because their enemies had already shown a willingness to go after her when she had been tucked away.

# CHAPTER EIGHT

She never thought she would be missing her home in Pelham Manor and the solitude it offered because how stir crazy she had become, but Sabrina needed a break from being in the cramped apartment with her husband who had now got into a habit of treating her like she was disabled since she was pregnant. She knew a big part of it was from the guilt she knew he felt about not being there when she was attacked, but she held him to no fault because she knew that he would kill and die for her without question. She knew that their lifestyle came with these risks. She was happy that her survival instincts and training had proven true that day and the worst outcome had been avoided.

Nonetheless, she had convinced her husband to take them all to the Bronx Zoo now that spring had came in and temperatures were a lot more favorable. For the pass two days her little sister-in-law had been staying with them. Marie was so beautiful and smart for a ten year old girl. She never cease to amaze her with how perceptive she was because there was no hiding anything from that little girl who had somehow figured out the big secret. Now sworn to secrecy, Marie couldn't stop showing her overjoy at the prospect at being an aunt times two. She had been the real reason that Genuine had agreed to take them all to the zoo because he couldn't deny his baby sister. Sabrina found it cute to watch Marie have her way with her big brother who it could clearly be seen that she idolized.

Things were still crazy in the South Bronx especially inside Mott Haven because her tribe was still in a bloody war with the Los Arañas who she wished she could take out in one fail swoop. They were back-and-forth with them and it wasn't looking like no end was in sight. This small gang was living up to its name and were every bit as deadly and clever as a cluster of spiders that were catching her tribe in their web of deception. They were terrorizing the streets with their brand of murder and mayhem. Nevertheless, her tribe was up to the task because they were every bit as willing to kill and maim their most hated rivals. Her nation had built up a fierce reputation wherever they went to have a knack for brutality when necessary that made most rivals crumble under the pressure applied on them. Her nation was one of a kind too because it was one of the only that had full female members who were just as deadly as their male brethren. Her small net of Queens were no joke when it came to protecting the things they loved the most.

"Big sis," Marie yelled from the living room where she was watching Saturday morning cartoons with her nephew.

"Yes," Sabrina said as she came out her bedroom.

"What time are we going to zoo?" Marie asked as she was finishing up the big bowl of Fruity Pebbles and then making sure to drink the flavorful milk.

"Your brother should be back before noon, so around one o'clock. Believe me, I'm just as anxious as you to go stretch my legs and see some beautiful elephants and my personal favorite, the elegant lionesses," Sabrina said as she bent over to scoop up her baby boy who had ran to her as soon as he saw her.

"Yes, the lionesses are my favorite because I'm a young one. I can't wait to become a Queen like you big sis," Marie said looking at Sabrina with her big beautiful light brown eyes looking like a mini female version of her brother.

"Aww, mamacita, you sure are a lioness as well and you are going to be a fierce and beautiful Queen because you are already a strong and beautiful princess," Sabrina said as she wiped the little bit of milk that Marie had on her chin.

The ride to the Bronx Zoo which was located in the West Bronx didn't take that long to get there. Her husband had invited a few of their soldiers to bring their families with them, so they pulled up with an entourage of thirty people which also made them look way less suspicious because she knew that everyone of these soldiers accompanying them were the ones handpicked by their new Cacique Mario as the most loyal. Therefore, she knew that they wouldn't hesitate to meet any threat with deadly force to protect their Inca and his family.

Her little sister-in-law was awestruck by how big and beautiful the Bronx Zoo was which always amazed her as well. Sabrina had only been to this zoo twice before because she rarely came this way. She didn't know how much she loved nature being a big city girl until she was around all these beautiful animals. All of her upbringing had been in a concrete jungle filled with a different type of animal that was more vicious than any that were on display in their exhibits that tried to mimic their natural habitats. The visit was made sweeter by the fact that there were other kids tagging along to keep both her son and little sister-in-law company as they enjoyed the various sights and smells in only the way kids could, which touched the hearts of every adult in the group including some of the most hardened Kings who refused to smile because they were too afraid that it would seem like they weren't on high alert around their Inca and Cacique.

"Mi esposo, you sure are looking extra handsome today," Sabrina said rubbing her husband on the cheek affectionately. "Aww mi esposa, you are my world and I love you so much," Genuine said looking his wife in her pretty dark brown eyes. He loved her dimples and the freckles she had. He never got tired of staring at her and found himself always stuck in this absolute beauty who loved him to no end and gave him so much more to live for as he continued to set them up to have a better future than how they came up because he had plans set in place to keep them secured.

"Aww mi amor, I love you so much too. You are my world as well and I can't imagine ever living life without," Sabrina said as she started kissing him not caring that all eyes were on them. She heard a few of her fellow Queens who were the wives and girlfriends of the soldiers with them comment on how beautiful of a couple they were. She really appreciated them and felt the same way about them as well.

"Ugh, y'all are so gross," Marie said as she ran back from the exhibit where she had been making faces at the chimpanzees who seemed to have been entertained by her childish antics.

"Girl, you better stop hating," Sabrina said laughing knowing how her little sister-in-law could still get territorial over her big brother even though she had long opened up to Sabrina being his wife.

"Messy Boo, come here," Genuine said calling her by the nickname he had given her a couple of years ago. He hugged his beloved baby sister tight until she started to squirm because she had been saying lately that she wasn't a little girl no more, so this long public display of affection had become contrary to what she felt was the correct way to treat her as a big girl.

They all left the Bronx Zoo around five o'clock in the evening and decided to go find a restaurant in the West Bronx that could accommodate the size of their group. She didn't care what type of food they got either because she was starving and couldn't wait to eat something more than the snacks they been chewing on at the zoo. To keep the small bulge of her stomach hidden, she had wore some gold colored coveralls to match the big gold bamboo earrings she had on with a black tank top underneath to represent the royal colors of her nation. Most of their entourage had decided to wear a variation of the same colors including her husband. There would be no doubt about where they were from if they came across any rivals. However, their tribe had a very small presence in this part of the Bronx, so they were in unfriendly territory. They were a force to be reckoned with no matter their numbers. Rivals big and small all knew that there were hefty penalties for getting into it with the Bloodline. The West Bronx was not exempt.

Nonetheless, she was happy that the rest of the day went by without any incident because this was truly a family outing. They had chosen one of the classic red-sauce restaurants in the Belmont area where Little Italy was located as a place where they got a bite to eat. This was her first time ever eating at any of the Little Italy restaurants, but Mario who had been spending a lot of time in the West Bronx lately had suggested it. The day had been a rare one where she could honestly say it was perfect. She always cherished these moments she got to spend with her family and friends because the way life was for them, death was always one step away.

# CHAPTER NINE

It had been months now since he had originally put out a terminate on sight order for the infamous leader of the Los Arañas. Genuine had started to wonder if Creeper really existed because not much was known about him other than he was possibly a thirty something year old man who had immigrated to the United States of America from Puerto Rico back in the early 'Eighties. The rumor was it that he had gotten deathly sick somewhere along the journey to America after getting bit by a spider. While sick and out of his mind, Creeper had been visited by a mystical creature that resembled a very large spider who had given him the destination of where he needed to go to start his mission. This had resulted in him coming to the South Bronx and forming the Los Arañas gang. They had quickly taken over the Mill Brooke Housing Projects where Creeper had come to live with a then girlfriend of his. It didn't take long for them to build up a fierce reputation of being merciless with anybody who opposed them through purposely targeting rivals they knew were married and had families, hence how they became known as widow makers. This cutthroat attitude of theirs made it not surprising that they had dared to make a hit on his wife which he still didn't know how they had obtained the location of his Pelham Manor home.

Nonetheless, Genuine had just received some amazing news that needed his immediate attention, so he along with his Cacique were headed to an undisclosed location of theirs inside the Concourse neighborhood. It was a safe house that few knew about. They had been informed by Blade that the elusive Creeper had been injured and captured after being betrayed by one of his top lieutenants with aspirations of taking his place. They had finally got the drop on him after all this time after Genuine was starting to come to the conclusion that they would probably never get him. He was happy that Creeper was still alive, so he could look him in the eyes before he took the pleasure of stabbing him deep in the gut with his ten-inch serrated knife with the lion's head on the tip of its grip that he carried on him at all times. He couldn't wait to share the news with his wife that he had watched the life leave their most hated rival's eyes.

"Amor De Rey," Blade said as he greeted them at the front door.

"Amor De Rey," both said as they entered the house. "My twins, let me show y'all my gift," Blade said as they walked to a back room through a dimly lit hallway. Genuine couldn't contain his joy when he saw a small man with a very long Mongol styled ponytail tied up in a chair who clearly had been shot in the chest. The infamous Creeper immediately made eye contact with them as they entered the room. There was absolutely no fear in his menacing stare as he watched them look at him like he knew what they were thinking and welcomed every bit of it.

"So this is Creeper? From all the rumors, I would've thought you were a seven foot tall giant of a man, but I've been around long enough to know the smallest are usually the deadliest especially with spiders huh? I've waited so long to share a space with you," Genuine said as he closed the distance between them.

"You fucking putas don't put no fear in my heart because I'm a dead man already. I died a very long time ago and have been walking this plane as a reaper taking souls for my Anansi who brought me back to do his bidding," Creeper said venomously.

"You look very much alive to me muthafucka. At least for the time being," Genuine said laughing with Mario and Blade. They all found amusement in the fight of their rival. He also knew that his manitos weren't disappointed like him that Creeper so far was living up to his legend because rarely ever the myth matched the man.

"Fuck you Latin traitors because ain't nothing kingly about y'all. Even when I'm gone, my Arañas will never submit to y'all oppression," Creeper said.

"You got very strong words and you are right about one thing though, yeah yo filthy ass gang of spiders would never have to worry about being under our rule because we are going to rid the Bronx of every last one of you after I kill you first," Genuine said as he slowly pulled out his knife.

"Go ahead and do yo worst. The Los Arañas will avenge my death and worship me like they worship our Anansi who is waiting on me as we speak to reward me for all of my years of service," Creeper said never flinching as Genuine slowly started to press the knife deep into his gut.

"Cut this muthafucka up and throw him all over his turf to let his muthafucka'n organization know what to expect will be their end once we start invading their projects," Genuine said as he wiped his bloody knife off on the pants of a now lifeless Creeper who's death stare was every bit as menacing as it had been in life.

He left the house with Mario and went to visit the Webster Housing Projects where they had a meeting with TJ and Ace who were the leaders of the BBGs. This had been where they were originally getting ready to go to when Blade had sent word about Creeper. Consequently, Genuine felt real good like he had just smoked some of the bomb weed the Jamaicans always seemed to have in an endless supply. Later on in the week, he wanted to host a party in honor of all their recent success especially if the meeting went as plan between them and the BBGs who had really been smart in forming the alliance with the Bloodline that gave them opportunities for growth that they never imagined. Genuine ever the mastermind was thinking about deepening their bond to combine their might to takeover the Bronx because they were two of the strongest organizations inside the borough with a lot of the same interest and enemies they hated with a passion.

The drive up Webster Avenue to get to their destination from where they were coming from didn't take them that long at all. Mario already had top members of their tribe who lived in the Websters ready to meet them and accompany them to one of the buildings that was considered shared turf with the BBGs who could be easily identified by the bright red clothes they love to wear to show that they were members of the Bloods.

"Hola mi amigos," Ace said who was a large dark skinned Dominican man who had been the one responsible for getting Genuine to agree to start doing business together instead of dropping bodies.

"Hola mi amigo," Genuine said truly pleased to see his fellow Dominican who he had really started to like in the short amount of time they had known each other.

"Yo son, it's really good to see y'all niggas fasho," TJ said who was a light skinned African American man with crazy green eyes and long hair he liked to keep in braids with a red bandanna wrapped around his head.

They all took a seat to get to the business at hand. Genuine let them know about his proposition to partner up which would allow them access to way better prices on each kilo they got from the Bombers Tribe. As long as they committed their soldiers to the common cause, the BBGs would be getting the same prices per kilo that his tribe were getting them for and they would also be working more closely together on the distribution of the weight of it within the Bronx and in New Jersey where the BBGs were connected with other Blood sets. As a result, the charismatic leaders of the BBGs didn't take long to accept the terms with a few counter ones of their own which would open the doors to get their two nations to possibly find peace with each other on a larger scale because currently the Bloodline and the Bloods were on very shaky grounds with each other due to years of fierce competition for dominance over the state and region. Genuine, however, didn't have the authority to make a decision that monumental, but he gave his word that he would send word up the proper channels to the upper management who he knew he had sway with because of years of solid service.

The meeting ended with the leaders from both sides having a little celebration. They sipped on some Hennessey mixed with Coke and passed a few blunts between them. Mario who was no longer tasked with being his bodyguard due to becoming his Cacique couldn't help but stay alert even in the presence of allies because he knew the consequences of letting his guard down. Genuine on the other hand, played as if he was higher than he really was because he sometimes liked to see if his friends and foes alike would take advantage if they thought he was lacking which he never was. His Cacique knew him all too well and could tell that this was a part of the act.

Nevertheless, TJ and Ace being sincere in their wants to continue their alliance never showed any signs of deception. Their intentions were pure which made it that much more important to solidify the relationship between them and his tribe who was still having a hard time expanding into the West Bronx where the BBGs had a lot of territory and influence.

# CHAPTER TEN

---

The news of Creeper's demise had spread like wildfire throughout the Bronx and beyond because he had been both feared and hated by so many. The Los Arañas were now in a vacuum over internal beefs over who should take his spot as the head spider. Consequently, this left them and the Mill Brooke Housing Projects open to assault which her tribe had started doing without mercy making them dirty ass spiders take cover deep in their web which they called the nine buildings that made up their turf. Sabrina was very pleased with the progress being made, and also was happy that her husband had started allowing her to get back to handling her responsibilities of running the Queens of the Bombers Tribe who had been missing her guidance. They were really a sisterhood with a tighter bond than any college sorority. For the most part, they had been meeting up in her apartment in the Mott Haven Housing Projects to discuss things that specifically concerned them and their roles within the tribe because even though they had equal membership, there were still things that separated them from their male brethren.

One of these such issues were pregnancy because Sabrina wasn't the only Queen who was expecting. Word had gotten out about her pregnancy now that the most dangerous threat to them was on its heels in retreat, but she was well protected at all times because this was still the Bronx and they still had enemies who wouldn't hesitate given the opportunity to hurt Genuine. However, their alliance with the BBGs had helped immensely to strengthen their position at the top of the totem pole.

"Amor De Reina," the group of Queens said as they greeted Sabrina.

"Amor De Reina," Sabrina responded throwing up the crown with them.

"You look so pretty mamí," Cindy said who was a petite Puerto Rican woman with the most beautiful set of dimples that Sabrina had ever seen.

"Gracias mamí, I can say the same for you and the rest of my Queens because we are all head turners," Sabrina bragged getting nods of agreement from everybody presence. Since a few of her Queens had young kids like her Santiago, she had made sure they brought them, so the sounds of toddlers playing and wining could be heard all around them. This meeting was mainly with Queens who lived in the Southeastern parts of the Bronx that she didn't get to see too much, so she wasn't shocked that the room was packed because none of them would dare miss the opportunity to spend time with the pregnant Queen Sabrina who had become just as famous within their tribe as her husband if not more popular.

"You said that right mamí," Rochelle said with the attitude only a Latina who knew she was fine could get away with.

"It's good to see y'all. For some of y'all it's been a minute, for the rest it's nice to meet y'all for the first time," Sabrina said looking at each and every one of them.

"Likewise mamí. You are absolutely glowing. I can see that you finally starting to show," Baby Boop said who was a very beautiful curvy Columbian woman who got her name from looking like the luscious cartoon character Betty Boop.

"Yes I am. This baby is very active too. I can tell I'm going to have my hands full," Sabrina said rubbing her belly.

"We all look up to you Brina. You are such an inspiration mamí. I love you manita," Cindy said emotionally which caused some eyes in the room to get a little moist because so many really loved her and had pledged themselves to her.

"Aww, I love all of y'all. Y'all are my manitas," Sabrina replied standing up to hug each and every one of them.

They hung out for a few hours just chick chatting about the men they loved, their growing families, the current affairs of their tribe and nation, and made promises to keep in better touch. Sabrina said after she had her daughter, she would plan to come their way to hang with them to really check them out. This was what made her role as top Queen important to keep good relations within her tribe to help her husband run the tribe because keeping up with the female members wasn't his responsibility. They both played off each other which kept everybody in check for the most part. However, their tribe had gotten significantly larger in both membership and territory, so it was impossible to avoid internal strife with so many passionate voices around. She knew that there were a small number of Queens spread throughout their Bronx kingdom that felt they were more qualified for her role and few Kings who wanted her husband's spot, but these fringe members had so far been very respectful in their dissatisfaction. She never allowed them to get to her too much because they all wanted the same thing which was the continued growth and development of their tribe and nation.

Sabrina did miss her family in the Washington Heights because it had been quite some time since she had last seen many of them especially some of her female cousins that she had grew up with. These last few years hadn't been kind on their relationship which had caused a rift between them that she didn't think could be repaired. A big part of it had to do with their differences in allegiances because her old neighborhood was predominantly ran by the Dominicans Don't Play gang who had a rivalry with her tribe. Like many of their enemies, DDP felt threatened by the allure of the Bloodline which was winning the hearts and minds of so many Latinos wherever Kingism was being preached. Therefore, they reacted in the same way so many others had by building up a fierce resistance in hopes of stopping the spread into their turf. Nevertheless, her nation moved like an empire, so most of this resistance was futile.

---

# CHAPTER ELEVEN

Genuine had thought things would continue to improve now that the Los Arañas were no longer a lethal threat to his tribe's reign, but now they had been dealing with the police turning up their efforts to take down what they were calling the new kingpins of the New York underworld. His nation along with the Bloods were now deemed public enemies number one and two by the NYC mayor's office and NYPD commissioner. The Bloodline was already feeling pressure being applied in both Brooklyn and Queens, so he knew that the mayor and police commissioner had to be pressing for the Bronx precincts to start showing results in the form of arrests for this new initiative to take back the streets of New York.

Consequently, he had Mario start to tighten up their operations throughout the South and East Bronx where most of their activities were being carried out to distribute the dope they were getting. Genuine was concerned that this new police initiative could unravel all the hard work he had put into expanding the reach of his tribe and nation. His tribe was already considered the strongest in the nation in both membership and the wealth they brought. He knew that the upper management was impressed by his successes, and he was hearing rumors that there were talks of possibly promoting him to head the entire city which would make him the third most highest ranked member in the nation and the highest ranking member outside of prison. When he had first joined while in prison, he had did it to simply find some solidarity. He would have never imagined back then that he would one day be seen as one of the most powerful in the state and region.

Nevertheless, the law enforcement threat wasn't the only problem pressing his nation because for the past couple of months, they had been dealing with some internal strife concerning balance of power. His nation wasn't immune to the disease that money brought with it. This disease was very contagious and had throughout the history of man, ruined empires and noble causes. Its name was greed and it made man do some very unspeakable and dishonorable things to feed its never ending hunger. As a result, some of his manitos had started having conflicts with each other over the massive profits they were seeing from the drugs they were selling and the taxes they were receiving from the territories their tribes controlled. Genuine didn't like none of this one bit because it was causing divisions at a time when he knew that they needed to tighten up their unity to be able to face the onslaught coming their way. He wanted his nation to continue to prosper, but the growing pains were starting to seem overwhelming for everybody. Only those like him who continued to be true believers of Kingism hadn't wavered from the fundamentals that got their nation to this position of power. The thought of a potential civil war was sickening to him because he couldn't fathom ever bringing harm to a fellow King that hadn't broke their oath.

"The reports we are getting from our connections within the police department are very troubling to say the least," Genuine said to his most trusted advisors.

"Yes they are. We had so far only saw a few low level sweeps that had caught some of our foot soldiers slipping," Mario said referring to the police sweeping through their territory on One Hundred and Sixty-third Street and Southern Boulevard where majority of their operations were street corner sales.

"I want us to start cutting back our daylight operations and corner hustles for the safety of night and dealing within the confines of the buildings we control. This would help us filter who comes in and out. For now I see no logical reason to continue to risk being out in the open to serve our clientele who would follow us to the ends of the world to get high. Let's work on damage control before this gets too out of hand like we are seeing in other parts of the city," Genuine said.

"Inca Genuine, what about our partnership with the BBGs and other obligations like our manitos down in Jersey?" Blade said properly addressing the leader of his tribe.

"I'm already touching base with TJ and Ace on being on one accord to survive the moment because they know that their organization is a target too," Genuine said pausing to look around at the five faces watching him attentively before continuing on, "And as far as Jersey and behind are concerned, its business as usual because we haven't heard nothing about them. The NYPD has absolutely no jurisdiction there. However, our main concern is that Brooklyn is looking real unstable right now between the police and the internal beefs. Inca Gordo is proclaiming that he should be our next Corona which we know isn't sitting well with the upper management especially the Corona himself. Then Inca Gordo is facing challenges within his own ranks because there are those who are no longer acknowledging his authority. I would back them if they weren't doing it based off greed and not principal. I'm getting with Inca Bronco tomorrow about trying to secure the Columbian connect which we all know was the reason Inca Gordo started getting absurd ideas in the first place because he is the one the Columbians primarily deal with which wasn't a problem till he decided to use it to snatch more power for himself," Genuine said shaking his head.

"Do we continue on with our assault on Mill Brooke because we can't afford to allow Los Arañas to regroup now we got them in such disarray?" Livewire said who was one of his top enforcers.

"On that, I don't want us stretching ourselves too thin especially now we got the police breathing down our necks watching our every move. I know the threat them muthafucka'n spiders present if they came back together. But we all know they have splintered into, what, like four different sets within their turf. They are now their own worst enemy, so we can afford to let them do what spiders love to do, which is to devour each other. Once the heat starts to cool down with the police having their summer fun with us, we will begin to move full force into Mill Brooke because I've long sought after this prime real estate for our tribe," Genuine said leaning back in his chair.

After the meeting, Genuine went back to his apartment to be with his now very pregnant wife. He had been most concerned about the safety of his family with all these recent troubles going on and had already started putting together an exit plan if they ever needed to get lost in an instant. She had been against it at first not wanting to ever imagine leaving their beloved city behind, but like him, she would do whatever was needed to insure that their kids were safe. The only people who knew about these plans outside of them were his Cacique Mario, Bronco, and Ace who he had really gotten close to over these last few months. They had formed a tight bond being the two most powerful Dominicans in the whole city. Ace had connections in the far reaches of the country that Genuine could use if he ever needed to. The last situation with the failed hit on his wife and son still haunted him even though he had personally saw to it that the head of his enemy was cut off.

"Mi amor," Genuine said quietly as he kissed his wife who was laying peacefully in bed watching TV with their son sleeping next to her.

"Mi amor," Sabrina said breathing in the masculine scent of her husband which always made her hormones rage.

"I missed you so much wife," Genuine said as he took off his jacket and shoes to get into bed with his family.

"I missed you too husband," Sabrina said getting momentarily lost in his sexy light brown eyes, "If Santi wasn't in bed with us, I would ravish you right now with how good you are smelling and looking."

"Dam mi amor you got me about to go put our baby boy back in his own bed. I would for make another baby with you if you wasn't already pregnant," Genuine said stroking her face and then gently rubbing on her exposed belly.

"The way we have been getting it lately, it would seem like we sure were trying to make another baby," Sabrina said smiling.

"Daaddy," Santiago said excitingly as he stirred and saw his dad.

"Aww my handsome baby boy," Genuine said as he reached over his wife to pick up their wobbling son who seem like he was going to try to jump over his mother to get to his father.

Moments like these were really what life was all about. Genuine cherished every second he got to spend with his family. He had learned in these last few months to not take it for granted because he knew that death lurked in the shadows just waiting for its moment to suddenly appear and take what was dear. He moved as smooth as he could in these streets, but he wasn't a fool to think that he could out run death if death ever decided it wanted him or one of his beloved. Nonetheless, he would kill any agents of death who thought he was there for the taking.

# CHAPTER TWELVE

It had been a little over a month since Genuine had had to make the tough decision to activate his escape plan and relocate his family. They were now staying in an apartment complex in what he had learned was called the South Side of Phoenix, Arizona. The environment was a lot more relaxed compared to where he had come from, but he had noticed that there was some real griminess about this part of town which in a sense made him feel at home. The two things that stood out to him the most about this desert city were the heat which was really oppressive and the space which was very impressive because he had never lived anywhere that wasn't overly crowded. It had been his Cacique who had helped him pick a destination because Mario had family ties in Arizona.

Things back East had gotten real nuclear before he had left. The two dirty cops who were responsible for the bogus gun charge he had did a year plus of his life fighting for before the case got dismissed had resurfaced once the Bronx had officially started implementing the police initiative to take back the streets of New York from those they considered to be the most dangerous threats to society. They had started targeting him and purposely following him wherever he went which hadn't really hindered him because he had already started having Mario run their drug operations out of the Webster Housing Projects with the collaboration of TJ and Ace. His Cacique was more than capable to handle these responsibilities because he was the most military-minded in their tribe.

Nonetheless, the real problems had started when he had learned that the FBI and the DEA had started a new federal joint taskforce with the NYPD and other local and state law enforcement agencies in the tristate area to combat new organized crime syndicates. His nation and the Bloods were to be the main focal point of this operation with the objective being to tear their organizations apart through building RICO cases against them. Genuine had never dealt with the feds before, but was very familiar with what they had done to the Italians. The feds were notorious because they played by a whole new set of rules which meant that they were known to take the gloves off to get results no matter the damage they inflicted.

The plan was for him to lay low in Arizona for awhile, so to keep the feds from being able to tie him into running the day-to-day operations for his tribe. Mario was the better option because he wasn't married or didn't have any close family ties in New York. This made it easier for him to become a ghost and insulate himself to make it harder for them to pinpoint a location and then keep watch over his movements. They knew that the feds had no problems with using the families of their targets against them. This was one of their favorite gloves-off tactics which was to break their targets' wives and baby mamas through threatening to take the kids if they didn't cooperate.

His nation was currently on its heels from all the pressure being applied on them. In other parts of the city like Brooklyn and Queens, his nation was in bloody conflicts with bitter rivals like Mara Salvatrucha who was proven to be one of their most dangerous adversaries ever. This along with both the internal beefs and law enforcement attacks were really threatening to unravel all the progress the Bloodline had made in the years since it conception inside the New York State Department of Corrections and Community Supervision. They had already lost their Corona through seeing him get shipped far out of state to the federal super max facility located in Florence, Colorado.

"Mi amor, mi amor," Sabrina yelled who was looking like she was ready to pop.

"Yes mi amor," Genuine said as he ran back to their bedroom to see his pregnant wife trying to walk to the door. Alarmed he quickly rushed to her side and aided her out of the door to the living room where their two year old son Santiago was playing with the toys they had just gotten him.

"It's time mi amor. This baby girl is for sure ready to come meet her familia," Sabrina said as her husband gently helped her sit down on the couch.

"Mama," Santiago said as he got up from where he was sitting on the floor in front of the TV to touch his mom's leg as if he sensed something was amiss.

"My beautiful baby boy. You are finally about to be a big brother. I can't wait for you to meet yo little sister because she's coming," Sabrina said as she rubbed her son's cheek who was just staring at her with his beautiful eyes. She was finally not going to be the lone female surrounded by pretty-eyed males who were the two loves of her life. There was going to be a female added to this list.

The drive to the hospital didn't take them that long because they didn't stay that far from it and knew exactly where it was at. This had been one of the first things Genuine had learned after buying a car from one of the small seedy car dealerships he saw on a street called Broadway Road which was not to be mistaken with the famous one back in Manhattan because the show he saw on it reminded him somewhat of one of the blocks his tribe had controlled. He saw a land filled with opportunities the more he learned about South Phoenix.

"Push, push, push mi amor," Genuine said encouragingly to his beautiful wife in amazement because he never thought watching her give birth would fill his heart with so much joy.

Sabrina gave one last push as she felt her daughter come all the way into the world. The doctor immediately scooped her up to do their quick examination which included getting her to cry so she could take her first few breaths before handing her wrapped in a towel to her mother for the essential bonding of the newborn with its mother. She quickly grabbed her baby girl and let her settle in her arms as her husband watched with so much love in his eyes which made her hand him his daughter, so he could feel the indescribable feeling that she was feeling from the touch. Their beautiful daughter Sasha Garcia was born on August eighth...

SAGA TWO:

# Lady Fierce

# CHAPTER THIRTEEN

---

## 2009

Looking at himself in the mirror, sixteen year old Santiago Garcia who everybody in the hood and beyond knew as Tru, made sure his outfit was on point because this was to be his first party he went to since getting out a month ago from doing a six month bid in Adobe Mountain Juvenile Correctional Facility. He was no stranger to doing time because he had now spent over two years in-and-out of the Arizona Juvenile Department of Corrections. Nevertheless, Tru was happy to be back in the hood where he could get back to chasing the bag while these bitches chased him, which was to be expected because females found him irresistible. He was a five foot nine, one hundred and sixty pounds of all muscle, light skinned nigga with hazel eyes that could make a bitch cum on herself just by looking into them and also make an Opp shit on himself from getting caught up in his Crazy Crippin' stare.

Tru was from the one-and-only Park South Nahborhood Crip which could easily be said, was the most hated hood on the South Side, probably even in the entire city of Phoenix, Arizona, but this also made his hood in his opinion one of the strongest because all their rivals knew what time it was when it came to beefing with the Aya which was a nickname for his hood derived from Aya Park located inside the neighborhood known as Park South. He was feeling his all blue everything outfit from the navy blue and white Chuck Taylors he had on his feet, his crispy navy blue Dickey pants, navy blue tall t-shirt, and he couldn't forget his navy blue rag which he made sure to let hang out of his left back pocket, so niggas knew Tru Blue the Loc was back and on his bullshit. Tru enjoyed keeping his wardrobe simple which gave him that real Original Crip vibe. When he wanted to be a little flashy though, he would rock royal blue which was the color of choice a lot of the hood homies his age had started to wear to make their Crippin' stand out from the rest.

"What's craccin' cuz? What that Nahborhood Crip C like?" Tru yelled to some of his homies who were chilling on his home block of Atlanta Avenue just off Eighteenth Place which was the signature street of the hood. The party was just around the corner in the Roesers which were a bunch of one-story apartments that were broken down into sections. They sit just outside of the neighborhood on Roeser Road. They served as one of the favored hangout spots for Park South niggas to get their grind on.

"What's craccin' cuz? Hood, you already know that my Crippin' crazy official," Guuwop replied who was one of Tru's closest homies and a member of his Crazy Crippin' Crew which had built up a fierce reputation from living up to their name.

Tru took a brief moment to look his homie over. Guuwop was slightly shorter than him standing at five foot seven. He was a skinny dark skinned nigga with short Mohawk styled dreadlocks that only he seemed to be able to pull off. His homie could always be found outside somewhere in the hood regulating or creeping with the most ratchet of Park South hood rats because he loved the drama they brought. Just like Tru, Guuwop was blued up from the shoe up, but was rocking royal blue because he said his Crippin' was king.

"Yeah cuz, I already know yo black centipede looking ass a C Rida fasho," Tru said laughingly as he did the Nahborhood handshake with Guuwop and the three other homies who were chilling with him.

"You ol' yella Spanish fly looking nicca. You always trying to sneak a shot in with a compliment," Guuwop said as everybody started laughing and nodding their heads in agreement because it was well-known that Tru loved to joke with the homies as much as he loved to get into it with an Opp which he tended to do a lot.

"Ha, ha, ha, y'all niccas just mad cuz these bitches love them some Papí Tru Loc. But y'all niccas going to the big homie Lil C Loc's party or what cuz?" Tru said.

"Cuz, I don't know 'bout these fur ball ass niccas, but you already know Guuwop the Bozo is fasho ain't gone never miss an opportunity to fuck a slut in her butt," Guuwop said seriously.

"Cuz, that's why yo ass a dirty dick nicca for real cuz," Ounce Loc said shaking his head, "But fasho the night is still young and I ain't got shit else to do."

It didn't take them long to bend the corner and make it to the section of the Roesers where the party was being held both inside their big homie's apartment and the courtyard that separated the rows of apartments that faced each other on the opposite ends. The Roesers were the closest thing Park South had to some projects, and they lived up to the unruly nature that was associated with living in majority of the public housing throughout the ghettos of America. They were also a very dangerous place to be in because it was one of the favored spots where Opps loved to swing pass and shoot at any homies they caught hanging out front. While he was away on his last bid, one of the homies had gotten gunned down walking back into the hood after a night of hustling.

Therefore, this was one of the many reasons why Tru and most of the homies especially those in his Crazy Crippin' Crew could not and would not be found without a heat for anybody cold enough to make a play for one of them. He had caught more than a few slipping on his lurks to know that somebody somewhere felt like they owed him one. He adjusted his t-shirt some to conceal the big black forty-five caliber pistol he had tucked away in his waistband as they entered the courtyard. He went to find a spot where he could enjoy the festivities while also being aware of his surroundings. The party wasn't quite packed yet, but people were still arriving and choosing to hang out in the courtyard first in hopes of getting a plate of the barbeque ribs, hot links, and burgers being grilled with a side of potato salad that Lil C Loc's wife was overseeing. He wasn't hungry, so he reached into the cooler by the grill and helped himself to three tall cans of Mickey's. He then headed inside to where the music was blasting and saw a bubble butt swaying to the beat, so he quickly pressed himself against it and wasn't denied access once she turned her head and was mesmerized by his eyes. She quickly accepted one of the Mickey's and started to back it up into him.

After about three songs of heavy grinding, Tru decided to get the fine piece of chocolate's digits once he saw she was both cute in the face and thick in the waist. He didn't consider himself to be too conceded, but he had been known to turn a female down who didn't catch his eye for beauty. He was feeling a buzz from the beers he had drunk back-to-back and wanted to get some of the fresh summer air, so he left the homie Guuwop who was getting cozy with one of the hood home girls on the couch and went back out front to the courtyard. The night sky had finally came in, so the only light out was from the courtyard lights and the fire cooking food on the grill which had the whole courtyard smelling good. As a result, he felt his stomach start to grumble.

"Cathy, let me get one of them hot links cuz," Tru said to Lil C Loc's wife.

"Boy, you can make yo own dam plate if you want some food. The only nicca I serve here, is my hubby. Shit cuz, we made the food free of charge and yo high yella ass want to be pampered too," Cathy said talking shit as usual.

"Okay cuz, I was just asking. You need to stop playing and hook a nicca up with that fine ass friend of yours and tell her I said stop fucking with them West Side niccas all the time and give a Nahborhood nicca some play," Tru said smiling as he grabbed a paper plate and made two hot link sandwiches with extra barbecue sauce dripping the way he liked.

"Nicca, you already know yo ass too young for Sandra. She only fuck with grown niccas and I agree she needs to stop fucking with them Dub niccas, but her baby daddy and most of her family from over there," Cathy said drinking a Hennessey and Coke.

"Come on Cathy. Cuz you already know I got more bread than most of these niccas around here and y'all what, like only five years older than me at the most and my seventeenth C day is next month. You already know I've slayed some of yo other home girls and I bet they had no complaints. Big bro tell yo wife stop cock blocking cuz," Tru said.

Putting his hands up, Lil C Loc laughingly replied, "Shit cuz, I'm not getting involved with that. Yo ass already know if you want that then the next time you see Sandra, shoot your shot cuz. But it's good to have you back out cuz it's been a minute since I last saw yo ass."

All Tru could do was shake his head because he knew they wasn't going be of any help. For the longest, he had been lusting after Sandra sexy redbone ass. She was a dime plus eight for sure and to top it off, she was a straight up hustler too, but she had long since moved to West Phoenix where she had been exclusively giving Dub niggas all her love and affection. For now, he would find something to take home for the night because he had went too many nights locked up wishing he could get some pussy. He got up and found the chocolate thing he had been dancing with still hanging around and easily secured where he was headed for the next few hours. If it was some bomb like he thought, then he might spend all night and some of his Saturday morning digging her out.

# CHAPTER FOURTEEN

The summer had been so boring so far for Sasha Garcia who couldn't wait for it to be over because she couldn't wait for her freshman year at South Mountain High School to start. She was tired of being treated like a kid by both her dad and her big brother. Yes, she was only fourteen years old, but she was far from being the immature brat she had been growing up. Sasha had already started to make a name for herself outside of being known as Tru Blue the Loc's little sister even though she knew her big brother played a huge part of why her Crippin' was being respected by home boys and home girls alike. The hood was getting use to calling her Lady Fierce because she had shown just how fierce her mouth could be when she talked her shit and then how fierce her hands were when any bitch felt they had a problem.

Nonetheless, she would never admit that the origin of her name actually came from her favorite singer Beyoncé's alter ego Sasha Fierce. She was a huge fan of Beyoncé because her music and style were both dope. Beyoncé was also a role model for black girls like her who had Latin roots, so it only made sense that Sasha honored her mentor by choosing a nickname befitting of her stature.

Once she officially became a high school student, she knew she would be able to put the stamp down that solidify her role as Lady Fierce to the South Side and beyond. At first, a few of the home girls from the hood that she wasn't close to had made the mistake to start making a mockery of it because they had been jealous of the attention she got from who her family was and how pretty she was until she had came at them so fierce that they hadn't even made a whisper of a disrespect in her direction. It wasn't her fault she was blessed with good genes that reflected in her coming from a well respected family of good looking people.

It was Fourth Of July and her dad wanted to take them all to go see some fireworks, but Sasha felt she could be doing so many more interesting things with her Saturday night than watching explosions go off in the sky. She wasn't five no more where she got overly excited at spectacles. Plus, Tru wasn't even home because he had stayed out all night after going to a party that he had forbid her to go to. The nerve of him to think he could run her life. Yes, he was both her big brother and big homie, but this didn't give him exclusive rights over her. She knew better, however, than to openly undermine him because he had ways to keep her in check.

A few of her home girls had gone and told her that Tru had been spotted leaving the party around midnight with some big booty female that wasn't from the hood which didn't surprise her one bit because he was just as infamous with his exploits of being a lady's man as being a certified maniac in the streets of South Phoenix. She also knew more than a few of these same home girls were most likely jealous that it wasn't them that he didn't leave with because they all had huge crushes on him. All she could do was warn them, but if they wanted to become another notch under Tru's belt then that was on them as long as they didn't talk shit about her brother. Even her best friend Karen who went by the nickname of Lady Loc couldn't hide the fact that she liked Tru even though she tried hard to act otherwise.

She had grew up with Karen and had a love for her more akin to being sisters than just friends. She knew Karen loved her just the same. Their families were close too with both of their parents being dear friends, so it wasn't rare to go on family trips together. Karen's mother was Puerto Rican with East Coast roots. This deepened the bond between their mothers who were two of the few Latin women that weren't Mexican in the neighborhood. Since Karen was an only child and Sasha had no sisters, their mothers had been very instrumental early on in making sure their daughters grew up thick as thieves which they had been occasionally from being mischievous. Therefore, knowing Karen was going to be there with them when they went to Tempe Town Lake made it so much better.

"Wow," Karen said as they sat down on the chairs that they had brought and watched the night sky light up with colorful explosions.

"Nicca, you such a child," Sasha said jokingly as she too watched in wonder at what was truly a form of art being displayed overhead for the world to see.

"Nicca, I don't know why you trying to front like you too grown nowadays to enjoy fireworks. I can clearly see the amazement written all over your face," Karen said poking her tongue out at Sasha which made even their parents laugh.

"I ain't fronting 'bout nothing, I'm just don't get crazy excited no more about them is all I'm saying, but that doesn't mean I can't sit back and enjoy the night with my family which I am for your information," Sasha chuckled as she too poked her tongue out at Karen in retaliation.

They spent about another hour or so just sitting around talking and enjoying the show. The day had been a very good one even though her brother Tru almost didn't make it up there in time to be with them. He had claimed something had came up that needed his attention which meant something concerning his crew. She admired his Crazy Crippin' Crew which made her want to start a crew of her own which she felt was a pretty good idea that would further help her gain more respect individually on her name without Tru having influence over it. Karen's aunt and uncle who lived in Tempe had came with their fine son Allan. Sasha had always had a crush on him, but he was a few years older than them and always treated her like he treated Karen, as his kid cousin. However, she was no longer the stick figure he remembered from the last time he seen her a year ago because she had developed some womanly curves that she could tell had caught his attention.

"Dad, are we still going to out to eat after this?" Sasha said because she hadn't really eaten nothing all day except a blueberry Pop Tart that morning for breakfast.

"Yes mi amor, we are still going. We should be leaving here in about another thirty minutes. You must be hungry huh?" Sammy replied looking at his daughter.

"I know her butt probably hungry because she ain't ate nothing but some snacks," Sabrina said answering for her daughter.

"Mom, I wasn't really hungry today. Plus, I knew I would be eating good tonight when we went out celebrating," Sasha said giving her beautiful mom a playful side eye.

"Brina, leave that girl alone," laughingly said Monica who was Karen's mom.

Their parents had chosen to go to a Denny's not that far from where they were at for their family dinner. However, Tru had been excused and had driven off in the blue 2006 Nissan Altima on twenty-inch chrome rims their dad had got him last year for his sixteenth birthday. It had sat in the garbage for over six months while he was away on his latest bid. He had gotten into trouble with the law for an assault he had committed at Arizona Mills Mall which had got him permanently banned for life from ever stepping foot up there again. The state had threatened to charge him as an adult at the time, but had ultimately decided to give him another chance to clean up his act. He hadn't learned though because he had stayed fighting while inside and was now back roaming the streets. He was her big brother and she looked up to him nonetheless, because he had schooled her to his Crazy Crippin' ways.

Their dad completely understood why his son was the way he was, being a street nigga himself even though he didn't like them choosing to be Crips instead of following in his footsteps. He still had strong connections back East with his nation, the Latin Kings who he kept in contact with through close homies he had grown up with. This was made even more evident every time they took a trip to the NYC to visit family where she would see all the people in gold and black showing up to pay him mad respect. Their dad also even wielded heavy influence inside their hood with a lot of their older homies who liked to be referred to as the O' Cs or Original Crips. A fair number of these O' Cs didn't bang Nahborhood though, but flew under the old CC Live regime which was when Park South was a part of Chocolate City that in its heyday had spanned outside the boundaries of their hood. The only family member missing from today's festivities was her aunt Marie who was her dad's baby sister. Her aunt had moved out to the Valley of the Sun last year to be closer to her Arizona family because she had grown far too tired of all the domestic drama going on between her and her then husband. Sasha loved the fact that she now had her youngest aunt out this way because they always had a tight bond. Throughout the years, they had always kept in touch through phone calls and social media. Sasha even had her own room at her aunt's whenever she went to visit which was often. However, Marie had become a workaholic since landing a job as a registered nurse at St. Joseph's Hospital in East Phoenix, so she was rarely at her crib located by South Mountain which was just a few miles away from where they lived. This was why she, to all of their displeasure, had missed the opportunity to spend the Fourth Of July with the family, but Sasha completely understood because her aunt had confided in her recently that she worked so much in an attempt to keep herself distracted from the ache she still felt sometimes from a broken heart.

Sasha had decided to go spend the night at Karen's where the guest bedroom could easily be called her room also, so she really had personal rooms in three separate locations since she spent a significant amount of time over the years there as well. Karen stayed on Twentieth Street and Carver Drive which was a short block with the hood park, Aya attached to its end. Aya Park which was also known throughout the South Side as the Mini Park since it was a really small enclosed area, was where a lot of the O' Cs and big homies of the hood liked to congregate for hood meetings and functions. Karen's dad was a part of the first generation back in the day to bang

Nahborhood Crip which made him an O' C. They stayed up late gossiping about scandalous home girls, trifling home boys, and what they thought high school was going to be like which was set to start in about a month.

# CHAPTER FIFTEEN

Tru was back in the Roesers again, but this time it was strictly for business because he was overseeing the trap spot him and his Crazy Crippin' homies had recently opened since he was back and at the helm where he belonged to lead them to the riches that were for sure out there for the taking. They had gotten a fiend to agree to let them use her apartment for a small weekly fee and quickly had set up shop. There was no stopping him this time from fattening up his pockets. He also had an opportunity to start pimping since he had these two older renegade hoes in their mid twenties begging him over the past week to manage them. They were heading all the way out to the blade in West Phoenix to work and swore all they needed was his presence near for protection. They told him that they would break him off the lion's share of what they made off each trick for his time. The big homie C Macc who was a gang banger turned pimp was trying to encourage him to jump on the offer, but what was holding him back was the thought of somebody potentially trying to pimp his beloved sister, and that thought alone enraged him and made him not want to get involved because he had more than enough bad shit already out there for a lifetime of karma. Therefore for now, he would let Sugar and Spice continue to stroke his ego with their pursuit because he had that effect over females where they literally threw themselves at him.

"Say cuz, why that shit ain't properly bagged up?" Tru said angrily once he was in the backroom where they held most of the work they were getting off before they went for their first re-up which was scheduled for the next week.

"Cuz, dumb dumb here was probably too busy playing *Madden* to come play his part," Guuwop said poking the homie Minion in his chest.

"Ah cuz, stop poking me with them rough ass fingers. Nah cuz, it wasn't me playing no muthafucka'n videogame that stopped me from doing that. I had to step out for a second to go check on my baby mama who said something about my son that made me worried!" Minion replied slapping Guuwop's hand down.

"A'ight then cuz, hope you got that straightened out with yo seed. We have to get this shit bagged though, cuz right now it's happy hour for these smokers. And I refuse to get caught slipping low on supply when the demand is high," Tru said as he started putting on latex gloves on which both of his homies quickly followed suit.

"See cuz, like I been telling u niccas, team work makes the dream work fasho," Tru said once they got finished.

The three of them then went back into the living room where three more Crazy Crippin' homies were already serving anxious customers. Tru knew that they had the best dope around because he was using an old connect his dad had been using over the years to send work back East to his homies in the tristate area. He had even got a half of key at a player price just based off his family name. Hustling was a part of his DNA because he came from a family of hustlers. His dad had schooled him in all the ways to survive in the streets, so he was a lot sharper than most of his hood homies his age even though he could be a live wire. This was why at sixteen years old, he had his own crew of five of the most loyal teenaged homies who weren't afraid to get their hands dirty slanging and banging with him.

Their spot was jumping so much that he was already thinking about expanding his territory deeper inside the hood. Once they got their re-up, he planned to look more into this to find a fiend's house suitable enough for them because it was six of them total in the crew, so two could stay back to work out of the Roesers while the other four could start trapping out of the much bigger location which would require more sets of eyes to keep it secured. This might have been his first time running his own operation, but this wasn't Tru's first time operating out of a dope house because he had grew up around them and had started his career as a hustler at the age of twelve in one before his dad seeing what he was up had started gaming him about how to make his money.

He really looked up to his dad in every way because he was the real deal when it came to being a bona fide made man in this street life. Tru had even branded his hood name from his dad who had been known as Genuine back in New York. Since his dad had been genuine with his, it only made sense that his son stayed true in all he do. This was why he was Tru Blue the Loc. During his early years as a hustler, his dad had learned how to be real precise in how he maneuvered which had kept him off the radar for the most part until it had got way too hot back East which had been a big part of why he had moved them all to Arizona in the first place. This was also why he had chosen to live in South Phoenix instead of some ritzy area where they would have suspiciously stood out to their boujee neighbors. Park South was hood for sure, but it was still a beautiful neighborhood as far as how the houses were well kept because the residents for the most part, took pride in keeping up an appearance. Therefore, the neighborhood didn't look all rundown like a typical ghetto.

"Cuz, y'all niccas hold down the fort while me and Blue Shiesty go to the Speedy Stop to get us some more knacks and something better to drink than these muthafucka'n Diet Dr. Peppers Guuwop dumb ass got off that fiend," Tru said.

"Cuz, I did not know they were diet. I saw the cases, so I gave the smoker a nickel. Cuz, I swear y'all muthafuckas are ungrateful fasho," Guuwop said shaking his head as he sparked a blunt.

"How yo ass couldn't clearly see diet wrote all on the label cuz? I saw it immediately and was like what the fuck. You taking these muthafucka'n bottles with you when we close up," Tru said as he and Blue Shiesty left out the spot to jump in his car for the short drive to Speedy Stop which was the convenience store that was heavily frequented by Park South niggas who could be found hanging up there all hours of the day.

It was a little after eight o'clock at night when they pulled up to Speedy Stop to see a few people hanging out in the parking lot. Tru and Blue Shiesty both made sure they had their pistols ready because even though Park South claimed this store as part of their turf, it still didn't stop Opps bold enough to occasionally show up to get themselves something to knack on and drink on too. One of Park South's most hated rivals, Vista Blood Gang were just across Sixteenth Street and Roeser Road where the Speedy Stop was located, so it wasn't really rare to catch them coming up there in all red thinking they could take over. This had led to quite a few skirmishes over the years.

"Blue, you still got that fake ID cuz" Tru asked as they were getting ready to enter.

"Yessir, you already know. It don't work nowhere else but here anyways though," Blue Shiesty said opening up the store and walking in.

"Fasho, at least we got it for times like this, but I don't want the homies to be getting faded while we on the clock. A lil later, I plan to have some bitches come through the spot for some entertainment," Tru said going to the aisle where all the chips were at to get himself a big bag of cheddar cheese Ruffles which were his favorite chips of all time.

While Tru was stocking up on the knacks, Blue Shiesty was looking over the liquor selection to see what they were going to be sipping on when their entertainment came through. This was something Tru barely did, mix business with pleasure, but he was still feeling starved from the lack of female companionship while he was away. The crew had been doing good lately since they now had way less idle time which was one of the reasons they ended up having to pop their pistols at any niggas acting up. However, it wasn't a time of peace at all for them because the hood was still beefing hell of tough with multiple rivals who needed to dwelt with, and Tru refused to let the other hood homies think that his Crazy Crippin' Crew had grown soft in any way since he was out. They took pride in being known as some of the hardest young locs not just in Park South, but in Phoenix period and that said a lot because the Valley was Crip City in his opinion. The blue rage coming from all the various Crip sets all over was the reason why shit was so hot all the time. This is why he made sure that his crew lived by the Crip Creed, "Can't stop, won't stop."

The traffic had slowed some since they been gone, but homies and fiends were still out in full effect. This was why the Roesers was the place to be when it came to getting money because it seemed like all of Park South came through there at some point each week. They had passed some older homies arguing over a dice game after they entered the courtyard where the apartment their spot was located at which was dead center in the Roesers. Upon entering the spot, Tru saw his homies Infant Smokey Loc and Baby Gator still serving while Minion was counting up what they had so far.

"Cuz, where Guuwop ass at?" Tru said already knowing the answer.

"Cuz said he had to pull up on something real quick that needed his immediate attention," Infant Smokey Loc said with a grin on his face because he knew where Guuwop had went.

"I already told his crazy ass to leave that bum bitch Ashley alone before she be the death of him," Tru said shaking his head because Guuwop really needed to stop letting these females get in the way of what they were building.

"And I told y'all niccas to hit me when shit needs my attention. This was something I should have known as soon as this nicca left so I knew we were a man short. Good thing this place doesn't require no more than two to run it, but when we expand deeper into the hood, we are going to be needing all hands on deck when it's game time cuz," Tru said making sure to fully secure the door again, so it wasn't easily kicked in if some niggas wanted to be on some jack boy shit which would be suicide with so many other homies all around.

"Yeah you did tell us that cuz, but I figured you was on yo way right cacc and would find out then," Baby Gator said.

"A'ight cuz fasho. You right on that tip. And I see the nicca forgot to take them nasty ass sodas with him. But okay, in about two hours or so, I should have some entertainment pulling up. We gone close down shop by ten, so we can get all our mula and whatever work we still have put up cuz I don't want these bitches seeing anything and getting stupid ideas that's gone get their trifling asses blown away if they try it," Tru said putting the knacks on the dining room table and going down the hallway towards the bathroom to take the piss he had been holding for the last thirty minutes.

By the time the entertainment pulled up, Tru and his crew had sold out of what they had brought with them for the night and had got the spot ready to receive their guests. Their entertainment showed up in the form of five hood rats from the Aya who were very familiar with Tru and his Crazy Crippin' Crew's reputation. It could easily be said they were groupies who wanted to show that they were the most down in the fan club, so Tru being the Mack he was had took full advantage of this admiration by inviting them over to hang out and get their backs blown out for a few hours. Park South did have some of the finest females on the whole South Side. This was why they also had a high rate of catching niggas out of bounds who knew they weren't suppose to be in the hood, but risked it anyways all for a chance to get some of the best pussy Phoenix had to offer.

# CHAPTER SIXTEEN

The day of their first re-up had came and Tru couldn't help but feel a little nervous because he was suppose to make a proposal to increase his crew's biweekly amount from a half of key to two whole ones since they were going to expand their operations. He had yet to find a spot deeper in the hood suitable for their trapping needs, but was confident anyways that something would shake for them which it always did. He knew that at the least they could also start to employ some of the other homies their age to curve serve too since in parts of the hood it was still a thing. This came at cutting more people in which lower the profit margin, but it still gave them a chance to put more money in their pockets. The biggest risk wasn't the lower profit margins, it was trusting other homies outside their immediate circle to come through and not be on the bullshit that the homies were known to be on.

Their connect wasn't somebody that Tru would normally deal with since he was from Broadway Gangstas which was one of Park South's most hated rivals, but this was business. Plus, he wasn't the typical street nigga that Tru was accustomed to banging on anyways. This was an living legend that was both feared and respected throughout the South Side and beyond. It had been pure chance that Tru had connected with him since his dad had officially retired a few years back from shipping major work to the East Coast after Bronco who was one of his dad's oldest and dearest homies had gotten killed in Connecticut. Tru had been locked up with one of O' G Jigsaw's nephews who banged Park South and had gotten word to him about his plans upon release. O' G Jigsaw had immediately received him with open arms once he recognized Tru as the son of Genuine. He had fronted Tru the half of key to start his enterprise with and now Tru had both the money to pay for the front and a whole one. If his proposal was accepted then he planned to buy one and get the other fronted to them.

Nevertheless, the meeting was at least being held in neutral territory that neither hood had any claim to. Really no hood at all. They were technically still in South Phoenix, but the Pointe South Mountain Resort was on the end of the borders of Phoenix heading into the city of Tempe. It was really one of the nicest places on the South Side because it was really a hotel and resort where people with some nice pocket change could come and get pampered a safe distance from the madness happening just a few miles down Baseline Road.

"Greetings Mr. Garcia and Mr. Johnson," O' G Jigsaw formally said as Tru and his homie Baby Gator walked into the huge hotel room.

"Salutations to you too Mr. Rockford," Tru replied because for some odd reason O' G Jigsaw liked to address and be addressed by last names, but he was next level and had been in the game for a very long time.

"Come," O' G Jigsaw said as he walked them to the living room.

Since O' G Jigsaw liked to small talk for a bit before he allowed business to be conducted, they all sat down on the couch while his bodyguards stayed in their post throughout the room. He offered them some refreshments which they accepted with haste. Tru knew it was an honor to have this top tier hustler deal directly with him, a rookie in the game. However, he knew O' G Jigsaw was most likely feeling him out to see if he was worth the effort to groom. He also knew that they would have to go to another undisclosed location to pick up the dope which was why he left the money in the car with Infant Smokey Loc and Minion. Guuwop and Blue Shiesty were left behind to keep eyes and ears in the hood while they were away. Tru had also had to get on Guuwop the other day for getting too high off sherm and being incompatible of handling his duties at the trap spot. For now, Tru was going to limit Guuwop's responsibilities, but his latest fuck ups were threatening their expansion efforts because they were a man short without him.

"So Tru, how has your family been? I haven't spoken to your father in what seem like ages," O' G Jigsaw said sitting all the way back with his legs crossed.

Looking at O' G Jigsaw who was draped in the finest designer clothes with an icy platinum Cuban link on his neck with a stainless steel Rolex Submariner Circa 1969 watch on his wrist and a diamond studded pinky ring on his left hand. He was a lot more flashy than Tru's dad had ever been, but his longevity in the game that few lasted in attested to it just being towards his fashion sense and not his business which seemed to be real low key with a lot of precaution. Tru didn't think having large amounts of wealth would ever change his like of the simple look because he felt he didn't need to wear the top designer clothes and jewelry to look good. His hazel eyes and natural good looks alone were enough to make him high end. Nevertheless, he did desire the finer things in life like being able to do what he wanted to do when he wanted to do it without worrying about if he could afford it. Yes his parents were well off and ran a few small businesses that his dad had been smart enough to invest his hustle money into to keep residual capital flowing, but Tru wanted that Bill Gates money where he could buy a whole island if he wanted to just to let all his family have private homes there.

"Mi familia doing pretty good O' G. My mom has been talking about us taking a trip to the Dominican Republic later in the year for the holidays to visit our relatives out there. And pops is still working a lot settling into his square life nowadays while my lil sis is rapidly growing up," Tru replied leaning back as well getting comfortable because he knew that they were as safe as can be around O' G Jigsaw who he knew had mad love and respect for his dad, so he extended that love towards his seed.

"Okay, that's good to hear y'all doing good. What about you and your homies? How are things going for the Crazy Crippin' Crew?" O' G Jigsaw said.

"Well we are still building up and really getting use to getting to the bag in a major way. We have really taking advantage of the opportunity you have given us," Tru said knowingly that the small talk was over and it was time to discuss the business at hand.

"Okay, I see y'all can successfully move a half of a key in a timely manner," O' G Jigsaw said.

"Yes we can and I feel we could move more once we get a second spot," Tru said opening up for the proposal.

"So you're saying y'all are already ready to move more weight?" O' G Jigsaw asked curiously.

"Yes we can. I have what I owe for the half and enough to cop a whole, but I was wondering if we could get fronted another whole on top of that one," Tru said finally proposing what he wanted.

"Well, I do see y'all having major potential Tru, but I've been in this game a very long time. And that comes with some wisdom I have to pass on to you. Right now I don't feel y'all are quite ready to handle that volume. Allow yourself a little more time to get y'all first spot locked in and your crew all the way on board. Plus, I know y'all still caught up in the hood dramas. Yes, you already know I got eyes and ears everywhere including in the Aya," O' G Jigsaw said looking at both Tru and Baby Gator.

Tru took a moment to reflect on the wise words just spoken. Even though they weren't getting exactly what they wanted, he knew that they had got exactly what they needed which was some game to build off. He still felt they were ready to step it up, but also knew they still had some things to adjust. One of them was getting Guuwop to get his shit together which was seeming like a tall task, but he was a member of the crew for a reason and Tru had mad love and respect for the Bozo who was known to act a fool if somebody crossed him or somebody he loved. They left the spot and was told that they had their re-up waiting on them in a car that was parked in the parking lot of

Fry's Electronics which was a little down the way from where they were at going in the direction they needed to go to get back to their stomping grounds. Nonetheless, they were gifted with this kilo on the house and were told just to give the money they had for the half. O' G Jigsaw had said he expected big things from Tru and his young crew, but only time would tell if they were able to live up to them.

"Cuz, that shit was intense," Baby Gator said as they were back in the car pulling out on to Baseline Road.

"Yeah only thing cuz we are minor league playaz dealing with a real major league boss," Tru said seriously to all his homies in the car so they fully understood that this wasn't no play time hustling they were doing.

"Cuz, I take my grind seriously and I'm with you hood on getting to this bag. Shit I know we are dealing with a boss just off all the shit we have to go through to deal with him," Infant Smokey Loc said referring to having to wait till the day of the meeting to find out where it was going to be held and then having to leave their heats in the car before they were allowed entry.

They did as instructed by going to Fry's Electronics. Infant Smokey Loc used the key they got to unlock the trunk and grab the grocery bag that held what they had came for. Then as instructed, they simply opened up the driver's side door and threw the set of keys under the car seat before hopping back into their ride and pulling off. Everybody was thrilled to be back on with extra money, but Tru knowing this was a test to see if they were going to get careless, told them that they were going to keep that money to put with their next re-up because by then he planned to show that they were indeed ready to expand.

---

# CHAPTER SEVENTEEN

Sasha was chilling with her mom and aunt getting both a pedicure and manicure. They were having a spa day just for the ladies which was cool with her because she would never turn down an opportunity to get pampered. It had been awhile since all three of them had a spa day because her aunt was always working, so this was an added treat to have her there as well with them. They were more than halfway out of July which meant that the school year was just around the corner. She was happy to become a freshman finally because it would improve her social standings, but she wasn't too big on doing all the difficult schoolwork that she knew was going to be required of her.

"Hija, I'm jealous of how pretty your feet look," Sabrina said.

"Mamí, you know your feet look good," Sasha said watching as her mom get her toenails and fingernails painted pink with white tips.

"Sassy, why you lying to your mom when we all know she got some feet like a Flintstone," Marie said jokingly calling her niece by the special name she gave her.

"Manita, I know you ain't talking with them dogs of yours," Sabrina said to her always got jokes sister-in-law.

"Then it's true, we both got 'em and these poor ladies having to work hard to beautify them," Marie said as they all laughed at her antics even the beauticians had to stop working in order not to mess up the amazing jobs they were doing.

"Tia you are so loca for real," Sasha said laughing uncontrollably.

Sasha looked at the beautiful older women who were to her right and left. Both didn't look nowhere near their ages at all. Her mother who didn't have the colored eyes that her kids had inherited since they got them from their father's side, was still breathtakingly beautiful with her honey colored skin, long jet-black wavy hair currently in straight back braids, and ageless pretty face with the brightest smile that Sasha had ever seen. It could easily be said that her mom couldn't be her mom because she looked to be in her mid twenties. Her aunt was a little darker than her mom like her brother who was Sasha's dad. Her complexion was more mocha colored or caramel, and just like her brother, she had light brown eyes that really complemented the tone of her skin. She had recently dyed the tips of her originally jet-black hair light brown to go with her eyes which really brought out the absolute beauty of her since she reminded Sasha of some beauty queen like a Ms. Dominican Republic. Her aunt was barely ten years older than her niece, so at times they acted more like sisters. Just like most of the women on either side of their family, both her mom and aunt were short in stature, but made up for it in curves.

After spending most of their morning and afternoon getting pampered, her mom took them all to Chandler Fashion Square since they were already in the East Valley for a little shopping spree. Her mom said it was justified because she wanted her daughter all the way on point when she started her freshman year at South. Nonetheless, one thing Sasha wasn't lacking in was her wardrobe because she still had clothes, shoes, belts, and hats that were exclusive from all their trips back to New York to visit, but she would never deny her mom the pleasure of making sure her daughter was so stylish that every female who wasn't her home girl look upon her with envy while their boyfriends got into trouble from their jaws dropping. She smiled though because both her mom and aunt repeatedly tried with no success to get her to stop picking things mainly that were blue, but she could never go wrong with this beautiful color that had so many amazing shades to it.

"Mamí and tia, I really enjoyed myself with y'all today," Sasha said as they were headed back to South Phoenix after a full day of ladies only.

"Aww, hija, I really did too. We don't get to do this enough with yo tia always working and working. I be like girl I feel you on getting to that big bag because I know those paychecks be huge, but I don't want you to burn out and burn through life," Sabrina said glancing at her sister-in-law who was sitting next to her in the front passenger seat with her daughter sitting in the middle backseat.

"I hear you manita, but you know what I been through with Francisco cheating, woman abusing ass and I try to just keep my mind busy nowadays. The money stacking in the bank is just a plus I won't complain about," Marie said seriously.

"Yes, his sorry ass did put you through a lot sweetheart. He ain't deserve a second of yo time. An ounce of yo love and affection because all he gave you in return were broken promises and a broken heart," Sabrina said emotionally as she grabbed her sister-in-law's left hand with her right.

"I know manita, but when I was in love with him, I loved him with my entire being. And now we are through, I feel something empty inside which I don't know if I will ever fill. That nigga took a part of me and I want it back," Marie said with tears flowing down her pretty face causing her eyeliner to start to streak.

"Trust me, you will find love again and this time it will be yo real love," Sabrina said squeezing Marie's hand reassuringly before putting her hand back on the steering wheel.

The rest of drive was sat in silence as the three women let their tears cleanse the hurt that they felt for what Marie had been through and was still struggling to heal from. Sasha loved her aunt so much and really looked up to her because like her mom, her aunt was a strong woman who was a role model. However, they made sure to teach her that strength still could be found in moments of vulnerability because the strongest of people were the ones not afraid to show their emotions.

# CHAPTER EIGHTEEN

July was almost over which meant he was going to be expected to go back to South Mountain High School to attend his junior year. While away he had been able to keep up with his schoolwork through attending the high school Adobe Mountain Juvenile Correctional Facility offered to all their juvenile delinquents. However, Tru wasn't looking forward to going at all because it was pointless and would just be taking up too much of his time that he could be using towards his hustle. When he was locked up it was a way to get out of his cell. Plus, his classes had been coed because the neighboring juvenile female correctional facility, Black Canyon allowed certain classes to be mixed which Tru used to keep his flirtations on point. In his second week of being out, he had pulled up on one of the females he met in class there because she had been a cute light skinned thing with green eyes from the East Side, so he could make her own up to all the freaky shit she used to talk while they sat in class.

Going back to school was going to put a huge strain on the entire crew's ability to grind because they technically were all still high school students. The homie Guuwop was the only one sounding serious at the moment about dropping out which Tru was considering too, but he knew that his parents would throw a big fit if he did. They put up with a lot of his bullshit, but this may very well be the straw that broke the camel's back. The spot in the Roesers was doing great for business and they were still trying to figure out how they were going to open up a second spot deeper in the hood, but a few things in addition to their upcoming school year were making it look like it wasn't going to happen anytime soon.

Nonetheless, things had gotten a little hot lately because a few days ago, somebody had came through shooting on Eighteenth Place and Wier Avenue which led to one of the homies getting smoked, so the mood of the hood was angry because they couldn't let nobody think they wouldn't have to answer for this. The word on street was that some niggas from Lindo Park Crip Gang who they occasionally beefed with had been bragging about it. Tru already knew the beef between them was going to go nuclear again for killing a Nahborhood nigga. He was really thinking about getting his Crazy Crippin' shooters together to go get some get back, but had been told by the homie Infant Ace Loc that him and a few of the other hood homies were already plotting a murder mission now that the police's attention had been diverted elsewhere. He didn't particularly like having to potentially pop a fellow Crip, but knew these other Crip sets had a tendency to get beside themselves which made it necessary to put them back in their place. This was why his hood banged Nahborhood Crip so hard on these other blue rag hanging niggas who had the audacity to think their Crippin' was crazier. Park South would continue to be where Crazy Crippin' started in the Valley of the Gun, and they would make sure it was respected even if they had to empty every clip they had in their arsenal on Opp after Opp.

The grind never stopped even in times of war because fiends never stop wanting to spend for the delights they were being served. Therefore, it was business as usual for the Crazy Crippin' Crew who would continue to keep one hand on the packs they were serving while they knew to keep the other gripped tight on their heats if shit really started to hit the fan. The South Side was treacherous with so many enemy hoods surrounding them who hated how much Park South still shined bright through all the dirt they threw.

"Aya," Tru yelled to some of his homies who were chilling in the parking lot where he parked in the Roesers.

"Aya," the homies replied loud and proud.

"What that Nahborhood Crip do cuz?" Tru said as he shook hands with them.

"Shit, cuz you already know what it do. It rule the world cuz," T Locsta said who was one of the big homies that Tru really tried to mimic. T Locsta had just got out from doing some time himself and was back in the hood being a monster. He was one of Park South's most infamous members who had been known to slide through on a rival solo and drop him with no questions asked, so everybody gave him that individual respect and fear that Tru ultimately wanted for himself.

"Fasho you already know I know the world is one big bluetiful Nahborhood cuz and we run it," Tru said making the other homies throw in comments of their own to back up this statement.

"All this shit bluetiful cuz. I don't let nothing or nobody tell me otherwise either. When I was in the county cuz, I made sure to stand on it and had to make a few niccas eat their words for trying to test it," T Locsta said seriously which wasn't farfetched at all because he was also known to have hands for a nigga who only stood five foot seven and was heavyset.

Once inside the spot, Tru was happy to see that Baby Gator and Infant Smokey Loc were rotating the responsibility of handling the door while Minion and Blue Shiesty each took turns serving every customer that came in to make a purchase. A lot of these same customers would for sure be back multiple times before the night was over which for the crew was either around three or four o'clock in the morning if the getting was good and they still had work. Tru, however, had learned never to bring everything they had to this one spot. Therefore, the crew had stashed the work at Baby Gator's house while Tru held on to the money they made that was meant for their re-ups. He heard his phone ringing while he was in the bedroom counting what they made so far in the hours his crew had been there without him since he had to take care of some family business with his dad who had insisted that couldn't be avoided.

"What's craccin' lil sis?" Tru said lovingly as he quickly answered.

"Hey big bro," Sasha said.

"Cuz, you a'ight sis?" Tru asked getting a little worried because his sister never really called him while she knew he was at his trap spot.

"Yeah I'm good bro. Just checking on you cuz. Just miss you," Sasha said.

"Aww, okay lil sis, but you C knowing that yo big bro gotta handle his biz cuz. But on Nahborhood I will make sure I make time to chill with my favorite sista tomorrow, cuz I know I been all over since I've been home which is why dad made me hang with him today," Tru said feeling touched because his little sister was really his soft spot.

"A'ight cuz. I saw yo ex hoe too early today, and the bitch had the nerve to ask me how you been," Sasha said with attitude.

"Cuz, you already know I have many ex bitches, so which one sis?" Tru said laughing because he could clearly see his sister over there in her room shaking her head at him.

"Boy you need to quit with all that cuz, yo ass know I'm talking 'bout Sandrica crazy ass," Sasha said.

"Sis for real fuck that bitch. I saw her silly ass the other day in passing and the bitch had the nerve to try to flag me down. I looked at the bitch and kept it pushing," Tru said with a frown on his face because this was the only female who could say she had his heart, but she had twisted it by getting pregnant while he was away by some Opp from Vista Blood Gang which was a double slap in his face.

"Yeah the only reason I didn't slap the bitch for wasting my time was cuz she walking around with that big belly," Sasha said.

"And we both know if that bitch wasn't pregnant by no mutha-fucka'n slob that she wouldn't dare put up a fight against Lady Fierce anyways. All these bitches around here starting to C scared to fuck with the Loc cuz of my crazy lil sis making sure to know this Crazy Crippin' extents to the female version of me," Tru chuckled but was for sure proud of the fact that she was making the hood respect her status instead of relying just on his reputation.

"You already know I gotta make them respect me like they respect Tru Blue the Loc. My Crippin' stay crazy cuz it's Nahborhood," Sasha said proudly.

"A'ight lil sis, you know yo bro gotta get back to this bag. After I get up around noon I will take you up to AZ Mills to kick cacc for a few hours since it's going to be Saturday anyways. I will use you as my wingman like I used to do if you ain't mean mugging any bitch who want to holla. They all say we look like twins anyways which I agree cuz you get your good looks from me," Tru said.

"Okay bro. I love you and you gone have to pay me for my wingman services then, but it ain't my fault if bitches don't approach cuz my Crippin' got them shaking in their panties," Sasha said jokingly.

"I love you too mini me," Tru said laughing before hanging up the phone so he could get back to the task at hand. He had been keeping his ears to what was going on outside the bedroom to stay on point to what his homies were going through. The only one missing was Minion because he had the night off since they all had started rotating their duties. However, since Tru was clearly the manager of this operation, he knew that he better stop in on his days off as well to make sure things were copacetic which was part of the reason why he had decided to show up tonight.

# CHAPTER NINETEEN

The dreaded day was coming very soon and there wasn't nothing Tru could do to stop school from starting. He had already had to get with O' G Jigsaw about what it meant for the Crazy Crippin' Crew availability to grind since they all had parents who didn't play when it came to going to school and wasn't surprised to have O' G Jigsaw tell him to focus on school and hustle in his off hours by making up for it on the weekends. Guuwop, however, was really looking like he wasn't playing on dropping out because he had left home after getting kicked out by his dad and for the past week was living on Nineteenth Street and Chipman Road with some older out-of-town female from Chicago who had moved in a few months ago. He was telling them to follow suit, so they could continue to get paid which they really had started to see the fruits of their labor. Even Guuwop who was still wilding out smoking sherm and dealing with all the female drama had made sure to start to get it together enough to stack his bread which the crew split six ways evenly.

Nevertheless, all this success didn't come without envy because they had to check a few hood homies for thinking they were owed something. This didn't take much effort though because everybody knew that the Crazy Crippin' Crew was a crew of young shooters who would shoot to kill. Plus, they had the backing of some of the most reputable of big homies like T Locsta and what could be called the hood general for Park South, Lil C Rag who was locked up in the pen for knocking down two Opps a decade back. He was an O' C that other O' Cs feared and respected even in his extended absence because he still had long reach and influence in the hood.

Tru had gained heavy favor with the O' C before his last bid in Adobe Mountain by putting in some work that needed to be handle discreetly.

At some point, however, they were going to have to really choose either school or the grind because Tru knew that they couldn't have both long-term. He was over school anyways which was just a melting pot of bullshit and trouble from being forced to be in a tight spot with so many rivals. He didn't get along with none of these niggas who walked around in all red which was a color he hated with a passion and those wearing black because they were from Broadway. The only Gangstas he got along with were his green wearing homies from Hill Top Gangstas who's hood was located in South Mountain area. This was his hood closest ally because they had a long standing Park-To-The-Hills alliance that had been tested more times than they could count from having to ride on their rivals together. The only Crips they got along with at the South Mountain High School for the most part were from Seventh Ave Head Hunter Nahborhood Crip because they too rocked that Nahborhood Crip hard on any and everybody.

"Cuz, when you gone stop being on that bullshit and let a real Nahborhood nicca come through and cum hard?" Tru said talking on the phone.

"Tru you know you ain't ready for none of this. I got the best of the best on the South Side," Vanessa said from Townhouse Crip aka the Townies who Tru had met while passing through her hood because he had a hood homie who stayed over there. When he had saw her sexy chocolate ass, he had to stop what he was doing and make his presence known. His hood homie had claimed that Vanessa wasn't going to give him the digits, so he had to show that no female that wasn't his family could resist. Now he was trying to seal the deal, but she was trying to front and put up a little fight which he welcomed because he knew soon he was going to tap that.

"And I've been told I got the best of the best dick on the South Side, so let them meet. You know you just scared cuz you know I'm going to be having yo pretty ass in love after one fuck," Tru bragged trying to get her to bite.

"Cuz, I see yo ass super confident. I ain't gone lie. I find that so sexy on top of how sexy yo pretty-eyed ass already is," Vanessa said biting her bottom lip.

"Okay cuz, when you gone let Tru Blue the Loc come through then?" Tru said already knowing he had her.

"Tomorrow I will have the whole house to myself cuz my baby daddy gone have our son for the day," Vanessa replied.

"Okay, I will come through around one cuz that would give you time to have that pussy ready for me," Tru said feeling extra good because he loved pussy and there wasn't nothing better than getting some new pussy.

"Boy you so sure of yo self huh? Well this pussy stay ready, make sure that dick stuck on rock when you in my bed," Vanessa said hanging up.

While he was visiting the Townies, Tru had seen a lot more potential than an opportunity to get some ass. He had seen a prime opportunity to expand outside the hood which only increased his want to quit school before it started. The Townies really were a million-dollar spot ripe for the taking. The niggas from there were just looking for guidance and Tru was willing to bring his Crazy Crippin' Crew through there to show them what real Nahborhood Crips look like. The only problem was that the Townies also had quite a number of niggas from all over staying there staking claim to small parts, so they could end up having to gun shit down before they had a real chance to set up shop.

Nonetheless, Tru had his eye on bigger things than trapping all his life and that came from really being a boss by having multiple niggas working for him. He was trying to be the don at the top of the pyramid with his Crazy Crippin' homies as his capos running the various parts of the organization. He blew some chronic smoke in the air as he got in his car to head out to meet up with his crew who he was taking out tonight to a party way on the West Side in

Maryvale. They were going to unwind some and celebrate how good they had been doing. He liked the wide open space of the avenues of West Phoenix compared to how cramped South Phoenix was in comparison. It was the Wild Wild West for real that could be their playground.

Tru and Minion were the only ones in the crew that had cars, so they would be the rides up there. Everybody had their heats on them because niggas throughout West Phoenix tended to hate South Side niggas. They like to say that all South Side niggas were arrogant and thought they were the hardest in the Valley. Tru didn't contest that this maybe the case, but knew for sure that Park South niggas were the hardest out there without a shadow of a doubt. They had an Ak forty-seven in the trunk of each car with an extended clip attached as a just-in-case they really had to go savage tonight even though they truly just wanted to have a little fun without making headlines.

"Cuz, this party look like it's too packed already," Infant Smokey Loci said as they walked down the block from where they had to park.

"Yeah it do cuz, but we gone see if we can still get in. I see they charging too cuz," Tru said scoping all the activity going on around them.

They were able to get in after paying the little five-dollar fee and head to the backyard which offered them some space, but not that much. Everything was going good until Guuwop got into it with some nigga wearing red who was clearly a Blood. This made the whole crew get ready to take it to the next level because they were all trained to go especially when they saw that he had a few of his homies with him too.

"Say cuz watch yo self in this bitch," Guuwop said heatedly.

"Blood don't fucking fuz me," the nigga in red said in an equally angry tone.

"Cuz, on Park South Nahborhood Crip we can step out of this trash ass party and really get to it," Guuwop said.

"Like I said Blood, don't fuz me. I'm Alpha and on West Side Maryvale Bloods, we can do just that because I can careless about you or yo homies thinking I'm 'pose to be scared," Alpha replied walking with his three homies in the direction of the front yard.

"A'ight cuz, talking like that we gone see if yo ass can cash that check cuz!" Tru said just having to join in because he wanted to smoke these niggas which he knew his crew was feeling the same, but he also knew that they had to figure out a way to shake the nosey ass crowd who were getting excited and nervous at the sight of approaching violence. However, before he could figure out how to burn these niggas without so many eye witnesses, one of the niggas swung on Baby Gator who wasn't no little nigga. This made both sides start rumble right on the spot until other niggas who hadn't been in the initial back-and-forth exchange of words jumped in at that point, so Tru saw that they were now fighting multiple Opps. Guuwop pulled out his pistol and started firing which made the crew follow suit. Shit got even crazier after that when they all started scrambling and got back to their rides to see somehow through the chaos that they were a man short with police already almost on scene.

# CHAPTER TWENTY

Sasha found herself putting up her hair so she could beat this dumb bitch up who kept running her mouth. She had been a high school student not even a full week and was already about to fight. She had got into it with this bitch S Loca before at a party over the summer. S Loca was an Opp from the Bacc Streets and was from this female clique called Southern Belles that Sasha despised. Her home girls Karen and Anna Loc were already talking shit to two other bitches from Southern Belles who were acting like they wanted it, so it was looking like it was about to be an after school brawl.

"Fuck you puta," Sasha said.

"Cuz, I got yo puta right here," S Loca said who was a short darker skinned Chicana with brown hair she like to keep in braids.

"This Nahborhood Crip on mine cuz," Sasha said squaring up.

"Fuck Nahborhood cuz. It's Southern Crip on ..." S Loca was saying before Sasha took off on her and the fight began. They started going blow for blow before another Belle tried to sneak Sasha before Karen hit her in the face with a two-piece combo. Consequently, this sparked a repeat of their last fight which ended with all their home girls fighting, clawing, and trying to beat each other's brains out. This time they were just off school grounds which made sure they weren't at risk of getting expelled so early on, but the rage being put out between both groups was going to get somebody seriously hurt until one of the male spectators was somehow able to get them to let off each other because a resident of the neighborhood they were standing in had yelled she was going call the police if they didn't stop.

By that time, both Sasha and S Loca were on the ground scratching and screaming profanities at each other while their home girls did basically the same thing in various degrees.

"I hate them Southern bitches cuz. I fasho was punching that ugly bitch S Loca all in her face, so cuz had to try to wrestle with me again," Sasha said trying to clean herself up some before they got back to their hood because she knew that her mom was going to throw a fit that she was fighting again.

"Fasho cuz them bum bitches can't fuck with the Aya," Karen said in full Lady Loc mode.

"On Nahborhood that shit was fun cuz," Anna Loc said as she was putting the key into the ignition of her car since she was almost two years older than her home girls, she had her own car already.

"Yeah that shit is always fun to get in a bitch's ass who has it coming fasho cuz. I've been thinking cuz. I feel we need to get all the home girls our age together and clique up to take over on some real Nahborhood shit," Sasha said sitting back as they were almost to their destination since it was a short drive up Roeser Road to get back to Park South.

"A'ight. That shit sounds like a great idea cuz. What you got in mind though?" Karen asked with curious look on her face that matched the one on Anna Loc's face as well.

Taking a moment of consideration, Sasha replied, "What y'all bitches think about Nahborhood Honeys cuz we got these Southern bitches running around calling themselves Belles. Shit cuz, ain't nothing more beautiful than honey and we are that. Sweet when we want to be, but thick enough to choke a muthafucka out if they try to take too much of us at once."

"Cuz, I like that right there. Nahborhood Honeys it is then," Anna Loc said who was like a big home girl to them and came from a reputable family inside Park South as well.

"I like that shit cuz. Sweet and savory like honey. Okay we gone put together our clique and then make sure every bitch at South and beyond respect our get down or get put down in the process!"

Karen said seriously as they turned down Eighteenth Place officially entering their hood.

"My bro got his Crazy Crippin' Crew then there's the homies from Nahborhood Legends and COC which means?" Sasha said with a smile on her face.

"Bitch, you already know it means Cash Over Coochie. Most of them niccas broke anyways and ain't getting no bomb pussy like mine cuz they fucking these rats with no walls," Anna Loc said laughing as they pulled up to her house on Nineteenth Street and Mobile Lane.

Laughing, Sasha said, "Okay, what I'm trying to say is that some of the homies got their cliques, so it's been 'bout time the lady locs of the hood got ours and we could even start to invite some of our fellow Nahborhood home girls from Seventh Ave to join who we deemed worthy."

"Bitch, you do come up with a good idea every now and then, and I can honestly say that this is one of yo best in a long while," Karen said.

"Bitch, what you want a think tank worth of bright ideas. But fasho, I knew that y'all would love this one. Wait till we let the home girls know cuz we gone see all of them wanting to join immediately. Watch, pretty soon we gone be the biggest clique to come out of Park South. This is a Nahborhood world, so who gone C able to stop us cuz," Sasha said as she patted Anna Loc's pet cat who was purring and rubbing up against her leg.

"Operation Nahborhood Takeover is in full effect," Anna Loc said as they all started to come up with a list of home girls their age to try to recruit. Sasha was feeling like they were starting a sorority which in a sense they were doing just that because Nahborhood Honeys were going to be close and have each other's backs to the fullest. They already had three of the finest baddies as founding members of the clique because who could deny that Lady Fierce, Lady Loc, and Anna Loc weren't the female faces of Aya, so this was going to be more than enough to start attracting the cream of the crop home girls they desired. Now they just had to get some rules established because Honeys were going to be expected to live by them or be held accountable if they broke them. This would insure that they kept their standards all the way up.

# CHAPTER TWENTY-ONE

Shit had been way off since losing Guuwop. The homie had been wounded in a fight turned into a shootout a few weeks back and had been arrested because others had sustained injuries as well. Tru didn't know none of the specifics just yet, but he knew that they better lay low for a little bit from venturing far outside the hood while all this played out because they were present too which made them all accomplices. Therefore, he told the crew to really play the part and go to school while they stayed on their grind in the after hours which ended in shorts nights to be able to get back up in the mornings to start it all over again. The shit was rough keeping up, but they were motivated to put up a united front and possibly have some lawyer money for their homie's defense.

On top of all this, Tru's seventeenth birthday which was August twenty-first, was just two days away. It was going to be on a Friday which under normal circumstances would have been great because they would have been planning to go get their club on at Club Level in Tempe. However, now they were all on edge with all the uncertainty surrounding their homie getting shot then locked up and the mood was far from being a partying one. He found himself in class bored and uninterested in the bullshit that his teacher was trying to instruct. Not even the females who had been throwing themselves at him every day at school were able to catch his attention.

Nonetheless, his little sister was having a good time adjusting to being in high school. He did enjoy seeing her so happy and didn't want to kill her joy in any way by putting his funk on her. She had already started to make a name for herself because he had been hearing whispers about Lady Fierce, but he also had to make sure niggas knew to fall back on trying to make her their bitch. He would be damned to allow any of these niggas to sway his little sister out of anything. It was his job to protect her at all cost and he would pay any price for her continued safety even though she was tough enough to hold her own like he had taught her. Also, he had been hearing about a new female clique at South that were trying to assert their dominance called Nahborhood Honeys. This had made him smile because without asking, he already knew that Sasha was behind this as well. His mind had been all over the place lately that he hadn't even noticed how much she had come of age already in the short amount of time he had been home.

"Dam cuz, I'm glad to be out of that bitch for real," Blue Shiesty said as they were back in the Roesers. Wanda who was the woman that lived in the apartment they trapped out of was there as well. She had been on them about not cleaning up after they had left yesterday, but her real problem was that she wanted to increase the weekly fee she charged them because she had been seeing the heavy traffic coming and going from her door. Tru was totally against giving her greedy ass anything more because in addition to what they paid her, they kept her fridge and pantry filled with food and had even upgraded some of her appliances. She was acting up now Guuwop wasn't around because he had been fucking her as well which kept her ass in check. Tru or any of the other crew members weren't remotely close to being interested in taking Guuwop's place in her bed. Wanda wasn't that old being only in her early thirties and had a nice fat ass, but she was a ran through hood rat who liked to get high on the crack they sold.

"Wanda stop with all the bitching cuz. Yo muthafucka'n ass got it way too good to be complaining about shit. Yo muthafucka'n ass don't even pay rent in this bitch cuz you on section eight so shut the fuck up with all that nonsense cuz," Tru said as he walked out of her bedroom to head back to the living room.

"Cuz, don't be telling me to shut the fuck about anything cuz you on my daddy and you sure ain't serving this muthafucka right here," Wanda said pointing between her legs as followed him in nothing but a flimsy rob with her bra and panties on.

"Woman ain't nobody trying to fuck yo muthafucka'n ass and that's why you mad," Tru said shaking his head because he knew all along that's what this was really about.

"Tru come on. I know you be looking with yo fine pretty-eyed ass. Let a real bitch show you how real pleasure feel like cuz I know I can make yo young ass hard," Wanda said seductively.

"Bitch, I can cum harder with my hand than that shit you talking about. Get the fuck out of my face with all that. You know a nicca under a lot of stress and this what you pulling," Tru said looking real menacingly which for the moment put Wanda back in her place knowing that he wasn't one to keep poking and poking.

"Cuz, we only got 'bout another hour in this bitch then we gone for the night. I sure ain't trying to hear my mom's voice getting on me about coming home too late again, so let's get cacc to this bag cuz these smokers at the door ain't trying to keep hearing no bull when all they trying to do is spend some money," Infant Smokey Loc said as he went to answer the door again to service a pair of smokers that were regular customers when the shop was open for business.

By the time they closed up shop for the night, it was almost eleven o'clock. The night shift was still young, but it was a school night which they couldn't violate without fear of what their parents would be on. Some of the fiends who really enjoyed their product were still trying to get them to serve them all the way to their cars, but the crew regretfully had to turn down those wonderful dollars because they would then be stuck there all night if they gave in. The Roesers were still teeming with activity though because homies and fiends were still out doing whatever they felt like doing. The crew stayed alert because leaving with their profits and whatever work they still had always gave them an eerie vibe that they were being watched by hungry eyes. They were a pack of wolves themselves, but they knew that didn't mean that other predators who were starving wouldn't take a shot at them if they saw an opportunity. Tonight it was just four of them because Baby Gator had the night off. Tru immediately hopped in his car as Blue Shiesty and Infant Smokey Loc hopped in Minion's car. Together they drove off to head into the interior of the hood.

When Tru pulled up to his house, he saw his dad out front waiting for him like he could sense his son's arrival. He looked at his dad who was a very muscular man who really took pride in taking care of himself. His dad was five foot nine as well so they were eye-to-eye when they stood facing each other. Tru could see his dad's light brown eyes even in the dimness of the front porch.

"Hola pops, what you doing out here?" Tru said as he walked up and embraced his dad.

"Hola hijo, just waiting on you," Sammy said as he was hugging his son tight as they proceeded into the warm house to get out the chilly night air.

"Pops, everything okay? Mom? Sasha?" Tru asked starting to get worried.

"Yes son everything okay. Yo moms is asleep and yo sister is in her room probably on social media. Yo birthday is coming up and I wanted us to do something extra special as a family. I wanted us to take a trip up north to go camping and fishing like we used to do when y'all were little. Call it a small family vacation," Sammy said as he sat down on the living room couch.

"Okay, but pops you already know my weekends be hella busy nowadays with me having to grind all day to make up for the school days," Tru said knowing that his dad wasn't going to be denied because when he made a request it was to be respected and accepted.

"Speaking of that son, you know me and yo mom are all too familiar with living in the streets and the things that come with that lifestyle. I understand yo need to make a name for yourself and make some money while at it, but I wouldn't be right if I didn't tell you son that I never wanted this for you which is why I never indoctrinated you to Amor De Rey. Once I saw you getting more and more involved with the gang life, I knew I at least had to school you in the ways of survival in these streets. You know that I fully accepted and respect you as a man and as a Crip which says a lot knowing my organization's history with them back East. I just want you to know that I love you son and I know regardless that you are going to have to find yo own way, but please be safe in yo travels because as my only son, you are my legacy to pass our lineage onward into the future," Sammy said emotionally looking at his son with moist eyes.

"Dam pops, you know I love you too. I've always looked up to you and still do and will never stop. You and mom are my forever O' Gs who birthed me and molded me into the standup man I am today and I will continue to stand tall and proud into all my next cuz of y'all. Dam pops you got the Loc getting emotional, but I know even a strong man should know that there's nothing weak about sharing an emotional moment with somebody you love and care deeply for. I will make sure to go on this trip with my family and enjoy the life we have together cuz the future ain't promised at all," Tru said emotionally as well as he got up to hugged his dad tight knowing to cherish the father and son moment before going to check on his little sister and shocking her by hug her as well.

# CHAPTER TWENTY-TWO

High school had really helped her build up her reputation as the tough as nails Crip known as Lady Fierce. Sasha and her home girls in the short amount of time they had been official high school students, had really established themselves and branded Nahborhood Honeys as a clique of some of the finest, most down females around. Only a few other female cliques were even strong enough to be a threat to them, but these cliques also knew there would be strong repercussions for fucking with a Honey. They already had had a few run-ins with some of the other cliques to prove that they weren't to be fucked with in any way.

Nevertheless, there was one clique out of them all that Sasha despised the most and that was the Southern Belles. All their members came from a rival hood called Southern which consisted of the Front Streets who were Bloods and the Bacc Streets who were Crips, so they could be found both flamed up and blued up. These bitches walked around like they owned every square foot that they feet touched and were constantly mocking the Honeys which made for an even stronger rivalry between them. Their leader was a female named Twennie from the Front Streets who had a bitter history with Sasha's home girl and fellow Honey, Anna Loc. The two had fought multiple times throughout their freshman year and as sophomores had intensified their beef with the rise of the Nahborhood Honeys.

To make matters worse was the fact that Sasha had two classes with Belles in them. In her first period, she was the only Honey versus the three Belles who liked to sneak little stare sessions with her which she always gave them her fiercest Crazy Crippin' smug she had learned from her big brother. Tru had given her mad props and admiration for how she and her clique were handling themselves representing that Nahborhood to the fullest.

"Aya," Sasha said as they gathered up with the other seven Honeys who were both freshmen and sophomores because they had first lunch.

"Aya," said the group of Honeys in unison.

"Cuz, these Belle bitches are really starting to piss me off," Karen said seriously.

"Fasho cuz, you already know how I C feeling 'bout them bitches. They even got these Vista Bloodette bitches now thinking they the shit. All these bitches wanna gang up on us cuz they know they can't fuck with the Nahborhood one-to-one," Sasha said.

"Yea cuz, I can't wait to kick that bum bitch Twennie in her face next time them hoes get out of line," Anna Loc said animated.

"We gone catch these bitches slipping soon and we gone stomp that air they got pumped up in their breasts," Karen said.

"What's craccin' with the finest set of lady locs the South Side has to offer?" said a deep masculine voice.

"Moony Loc what's craccin' cuz? Yo ass got some nerve pulling up after that bullshit you pulled with me the last week," Anna Loc said already heated from thinking about her adversary.

"Come on Anna cuz you already know I only got eyes for you. You know you my main cuz," Moony Loc said grabbing her hand with a smile on his handsome chocolate face that said trust me. He was her boyfriend of six months. They had met at a party in his hood, Seventh Ave Head Hunter Nahborhood Crips and the two had hit it off instantly. They were inseparable until last week when he had been put on blast by another Honey who had caught his trifling ass all hugged with some female clearly not his girlfriend.

"Melvin, I'm not in the mood to hear yo lies right now cuz. You know I don't play when it comes to my heart. On Nahborhood Crip you know you fucked up, so it's on you to fix it cuz I will never ever be sharing my man with no other bitch and if you can't respect that then push off cuz," Anna Loc said trying to keep up a tough front while her home girls watched her.

"Baby, on Nahborhood Crip, yo muthafucka'n fine ass know I love you and I will make this up," Moony Loc said.

Sasha and the rest of the Honeys only looked on knowing not to get in between Anna Loc and Moony Loc because the two were crazy about each other. They were known to get into it then be all lovey with each other hours later, so it was best to allow her home girl to figure out her relationship problems on her own. Sasha on the other hand, wasn't really interested in any relationships at the moment because she was on a mission to solidify herself, so she wasn't for allowing some nigga to come in between her and her goals. Nonetheless, she got offers of courtship all the time from niggas in her hood, school, on social media, and wherever else she went because they couldn't resist losing the chance to knock the young pretty honey colored Dominican girl with hazel eyes who left an impression everywhere.

"You bitches stop being nosey," Anna Loc said walking back to her home girls who couldn't help, but notice how Moony Loc was able to sweet talk his way back into her good graces and finish the conversation with a passionate kiss with hands gripped on her butt before leaving.

"Bitch, ain't nobody jocking you and yo man," Karen said laughingly which made everybody else laugh. "Yeah bitch, we already know that's yo future baby daddy," Sasha said laughing.

"That nicca better get his shit together though, real talk cuz if he ever want a real bitch like me carrying his seed," Anna Loc said shaking her head which made her long braids swing side-to-side.

The last few hours of school flew by and it was time to officially be done with another day. Since it was Friday, that meant they were done with another week of school. Sasha was happy because this weekend was very special because it was her birthday weekend. Her fifteenth birthday was tomorrow and she planned to throw her birthday bash at her best friend Karen's house. It was only going to be through invite only to keep all the riffraff from coming and potentially ruining her event. She wasn't going to allow any party crashers and would have her big brother and his crew playing security to make sure of that. All of her fellow Honeys were invited with a plus one to bring their boyfriends if they wanted and a few of her home girls she was cool with not from her hood. She had also invited a few home boys she knew would keep her single home girls entertained.

She quickly gathered all of her belongings from her locker that she didn't want to leave over the weekend and left to go meet her mom who was waiting to take her to get her hair done. Her mom owned a hair salon called Sasha's Hair Salon located around Central Avenue and Baseline Road which wasn't that far from where her aunt Marie stayed. Her parents had opened it up six years ago in honor of their daughter which still touched Sasha's heart every time she went and got her hair all the way on point. Majority of her home girls got their hair done there as well. Her mom was an expert at doing hair, but nowadays only focused on overseeing her seven hair stylists that worked for her. There were only a small select few who she came out of retirement to whip up their hairdos which included her beloved daughter of course.

# CHAPTER TWENTY-THREE

The last two months of being back in school had been rough for Tru with trying to keep up staying in school while staying on his grind, but he and his homies had figured out a way to continue to do both. However, they still had to stall their expansion efforts because they just didn't have the time to stretch themselves any thinner than what they already were. They were barely able to keep their parents happy and their pockets happy with what they were doing.

Nevertheless, they still had a responsibility to their hood and keeping the Crazy Crippin' Crew's fierce reputation for being down for the Nahborhood that they loved. They had recently had to put in some work that their O' C Lil C Rag had ordered because he was one of the few who could call on them with no questions asked and get what he needed done. Tru had also been assisting with putting together packs to give to his O' C's wife, so that his O' C had the best work to make money to take care of himself and his family needs way from the pen. At only seventeen years old it could be said that he was already a seasoned vet when it came to this street life because he had been getting his hands dirty for years now.

The crew was still a man short, however, because his homie Guuwop was still locked up from for a shooting that happened at a party they all had attended months ago. The state had went ahead and charged him as an adult due to the seriousness of the incident even though he had been shot in his arm because they had found a gun with his fingerprints on it and the ballistic test was showing it was the same weapon used that hit two bystanders. They were still trying to keep up with paying his lawyer who was saying that with

Guuwop's age they had a good chance at mitigation, but at the same time the victims ages too had some counters that could aggravate his potential sentence. Things just wasn't the same without the Bozo present kicking up dust and causing a muck. Tru missed his truly Crazy Crippin' homie who always stayed CC Lit which was a phrase Guuwop loved to use which had become the crew's motto.

Things at school were also a little tense at the moment because the crew had an exchange of words with the Front Street Boyz which was a squad of four niggas from Southern Blood Gang. Tru hated this hood as much as he hated the Vistas because he didn't like Blood niggas at all and felt their color wasn't manly enough which was why real Crips didn't rock it. His hatred of Bloods was also the reason why he never went to visit his aunt Marie who stayed in a neighborhood controlled by South Side Posse which was a mostly Hispanic Blood gang with sets spread throughout the South Mountain area. He was a wanted man in those parts for sure because he had rode on them two times on the behalf of his homies from Hill Top who beefed with South Side Posse real tough over disputed turf.

"I ain't gone lie cuz, if these Southern niccas keep wolfing, I'm gone jaw one of them niccas cuz," Blue Shiesty said as they chilled in their trap spot waiting for customers to start coming through.

"On Nahborhood, me and that nicca S Dogg gone have to lock up fasho for all that shit he was talking like he can throw hands with me," Tru said thinking about one of his most hated rivals who he had been considering really catching slipping and putting him to bed for real, but for the moment he would fancy the nigga to show him that he was a fighter too.

"Fasho cuz, You know we got yo cacc. These slobs know what's craccin' when it come to fucking with a Nahborhood nicca," Infant Smokey Loc said with Minion nodding in agreement.

"These niccas mostly some lil niccas anyways cuz, so I ain't gone put much thought to them when we got bigger fish to fry like getting this paper," Baby Gator said looking down at all his homies

being the biggest and most imposing in stature amongst them standing at six foot four around two hundred and twenty pounds.

"I hear you cuz and feel you, but me and that lil nicca S Dogg
gone run that fade and then leave it at that if they can keep their
muthafucka'n mouths closed cuz I really don't like the lil arrogant
sons of bitches," Tru said looking at his homie dead in the eye to
remind Baby Gator that the pecking order started with him because
he was and would always be the craziest of them all when it came to
this Crazy Crippin'.

"Okay cuz, you already know we got you. CC Lit," Baby Gator
said knowing not to press Tru about wanting to handle his business.

"CC Lit," the rest of the crew said in unison as they got back
to the task at hand which was focusing on utilizing the little bit of
time they had to hustle on a Tuesday evening until they closed up
shop around ten o'clock.

The night had been slower than expected for them which
happened at times because not every night was going to be booming
with customers with money in hand. Plus, they were far from the only
spot in the Roesers which had spots spread throughout the various
courtyards that made it up. They were only able to stay competitive
because they had some of the best quality dope for some of the best
prices which gave them an edge over majority of the others. Most of
the other spots were mostly ran by homies from the hood. They had
two spots that had niggas who were on good terms with key O' Cs
that gave them a pass to hustle on Park South turf, but not without
paying dividends.

On their way out the crew ran into the big homie T Locsta who
was chilling with a few other big homies. Therefore, they made sure
to stop and pay their immediate respects to the homies who was the
face of Park South to the mean streets of South Phoenix and beyond.
The big homie as usual was being the hood politician he was breed
to be because he had a natural way about himself that made others
listen with full attention. Tru never missed an opportunity to watch

and learn to use in his own way to do the same with all the homies his age.

"I see my lil locs really getting it together cuz. Man I love the fact that y'all niccas got some drive 'bout y'all selves cuz a lot of these niccas around here starting to act like bums. This is why I C on their asses cuz I refuse to see any nicca claiming Aya looking like he should be living in a tent in the Zone," T Locsta said which made them all murmurs their agreements.

"Fasho big homie, you already know we always got to shake and move to make something happen cuz a Nahborhood nicca ain't ever 'pose to get caught standing still," Tru said on the behalf of his crew.

"Fasho. That's exactly what I keep telling most of these niccas around here. We gone start making these niccas yelling Nahborhood really live up to the Nahborhood standards," T Locsta said standing in the middle of all the homies with his khaki pants, shirtless with his shirt tossed over his left shoulder, and a big navy blue rag hanging from his left front pocket which made him look like the poster child of Park South.

"Just let us know when you need us to start pulling up on those lacking on this Nahborhood shit big homie," Tru said.

"Yeah cuz you already know we stay ready for the madness cuz," Baby Gator said who was well-known throughout the hood and beyond as a cold knockout artist.

"Y'all know I will. The O' C said good looking too on that last pack y'all sent him cuz. One thing we have to do is look out for all our locs locked up especially the reputable ones who paid the price putting on for Aya. Y'all niccas C safe cuz I then held y'all up enough. I know y'all got school in the morning," T Locsta said.

Tru hopped in his car as usual carrying the profits they had made that night. Things had kicked up a little at the end so they were able to make some money tonight, but Baby Gator was taking home most of the work they had brought for the day's grind. As seasoned hustlers, the crew expected this to be the case from time-to-time. They had hopes it wouldn't trickle into a slow week because then that would really put a dent in what they expected to pull in. Since their hours were limited, they already were losing and losing on potential, so right now they needed every dollar they could get from the time they had to hustle. Nonetheless, Tru kept a surplus as a just-in-case they needed for their biweekly re-up in the event of consecutive slow weeks which they fortunately had yet to experience.

Driving down his home block always seemed eerie at night like something was stalking him, so Tru kept his hand on his forty-five as he got closer to his house. For some odd reason that he couldn't explain, his instincts were telling him to be even more alert than he already naturally was being a prime target for so many Opps looking for an opportunity for major stripes. Therefore, he drove around the block past his house as an added precaution to see if he was being followed by one of the two cars that had turned down Atlanta Avenue from Eighteenth Place like him. One car parked at a nearby house while the other kept driving so Tru sped up when he got ready to turn the corner on Seventeenth Street. The result was the pursuing car did the same which made Tru speed up even more to create some real distance. He sped up to the neighboring street of Mobile Lane back to Eighteenth Place and bent the block back towards the Roesers where the pursuing car didn't dare follow. He got a good look at it while it sped up Roeser Road most likely all the way towards Twenty-fourth Street to get lost from the scene. His was livid by the time he made it home and paranoid out of his mind. He wanted to know exactly who had dared to make a potential play at him in his own backyard. If they tried again, he would be more than ready for them with his Ak forty-seven which would Swiss cheese the undescriptive whip they were in. It was most likely stolen just for the purpose of blasting him and dumping it right afterwards. Tru knew because he had been on the opposite end on a few occasions, so he knew that one day it might very well be his turn. He would make sure to give more than what he took when it came.

# CHAPTER TWENTY-FOUR

Things had settled down some for Tru since that weird night. He still didn't know who had been bold enough to try to make a play at him. Therefore, he kept his guard on high alert as he went through his normal daily activities. His crew had been in a murderous rage after he had told them about what had happened, so now they made sure to follow him home after their nights of grinding which he appreciated because he knew that they would dirt anybody at any time for having the audacity to try to take out one of their own. This was a proven fact that had been battle tested already with the shared spill of blood on more than one occasion. They weren't known as the Crazy Crippin' Crew for being church boys.

For the last couple of months since his homie Guuwop had been gone, Tru had started to grow out his hair which he normally kept clean cut to start his dreadlocks in honor of his incarcerated brother. The state had charged Guuwop as an adult and had him currently in some juvenile section of Lower Buckeye Jail located in West Phoenix. Tru had never been there before because he had yet to be charged as an adult himself. The lawyer they were helping to pay for was telling them that since the crime had been described as gang related, Guuwop and two of the Blood niggas they had got into with all were looking at some years because in all three people innocent bystanders who were minors had been shot in addition to all the endangerment charges the state was trying make stick.

Nevertheless, the way they lived their lives on this Crazy Crippin' shit made for a strong chance to end up locked up on the prison yard or buried in a graveyard. His homie was a bona fide C

Rida, so Tru knew that he was holding it down for the Nahborhood wherever he was at. He had set up a tattoo session with one of the big Mexican homies from the Aya who worked mainly out of his house tattooing most of the homies and home girls. When he first got out, Tru and his whole crew had all gotten Crazy Crippin' in big bold black letters going across their backs which they all loved to show off. Now he planned to get NHC going across his neck to let it be known without a shadow of a doubt that he was a Nahborhood Crip through and through. He knew all the homies would be jealous, all the home girls would be lusting, and all the Opps would be hating which would give him all the responses that he wanted because as he built his legend, he wanted to stand out from the rest.

His tattoo session was set for three o'clock in the afternoon which was a few hours a way. He still had some time to burn on a Saturday to make it the short distance to where the big homie Spider Loc lived, so Tru hit up his favored home girl that loved to give it to him whenever he wanted it. It was crazy that they were doing it under his little sister's nose who clearly had no clue that he was creeping with her best friend Karen aka the gorgeous Lady Loc who was a fine Honey indeed. It had all happened around the time he had first came home and saw just how much she had blossomed in six months. Karen had been over their house chilling with them like she was known to do and Sasha had left them alone as she decided to head out with their aunt Marie to run some errand. Tru had felt an irresistible urge takeover which to his surprise was the same thing that happened to Karen as she went wild on him.

As a result, they had been finding their moments to sneak off even if she had to ride with him and get it in the backseat of his car. Tru was finding it harder and harder not to stake full claim over her as his girlfriend, but didn't want to make things complicated between her and his sister because he wasn't sure how Sasha would take it. He wasn't big on being in relationships either since he never could be a boyfriend with so many females throwing themselves at him, but Karen represented that Nahborhood to the fullest and that in addition to how she looked was cake and ice cream for him. After he had spent two hours hanging with Karen at her house over by the hood park, Tru made the short drive on Twentieth Street to where Spider Loc stayed.

"What's craccin' cuz?" Spider Loc said as he opened the front door for Tru.

"Just on some Nahborhood shit as usual," Tru replied as he stepped into the living room walking behind his short and stocky big homie who had gang tattoos all over his arms and neck.

"Fasho cuz. Aya always and forever. You want something to drink cuz before we get started," Spider Loc asked.

"Nah, I'm good cuz. I can't wait to show all the homies yo latest cuz they all gone want to follow suit," Tru said.

"Yeah, you already know I'm going to hook you all the way up," Spider Loc said as they walked down the hallway to a back room he used as his in-house tattoo parlor which was hooked up with everything that could be found in any legitimate one.

It didn't take Spider Loc long to put another hood classic on one of his homie's skin. Consequently, Tru was more than happy with the end result even though his whole left side of his neck was sore. The tattoo had came out way better than he had imagined. Now he couldn't wait to show off. He looked at himself in the mirror and saw a Crip looking crazy at him with his royal blue rag wrapped around his head, his hazel eyes which had a blue tint to them at the moment, and his NHC tattoo still very raw, but ready for the world.

"Dam big homie, you got Tru Blue the Loc looking like the real C Rida he is," Tru said.

Laughing, Spider Loc said, "You already know you a C Rida cuz. Out of all the young homies from the hood, you and yo Crazy Crippin' are the most active fasho cuz."

Tru pulled out from Spider Loc's crib and headed to meet up with his crew who were waiting for him at the spot. They were going to be in for a crazy surprise when they saw his new ink. He hadn't told anybody not even Sasha that he was getting it, so he knew that everybody was going to be all over him trying to admire it. The black ink really contrasted on his light skin, so his tattoo could be seen from some distance. It was only a little after five o'clock by the time he was hopping out his car and walking proudly past homies who were out hanging in various parts of the Roesers. They all were offering him praises when they saw his neck glistening.

"Oh shit, I see you cuz," Minion said as Tru walked up on the spot.

"This nicca then went to the homie without us cuz and now stunting on us," Infant Smokey Loc said when he saw what had Minion so hyped.

"Y'all know the Loc had to do it cuz," Tru said positioning his body to the side so they could get a better look.

"Nahborhood!" Blue Shiesty said loudly getting the attention of others who were coming-and-going throughout the courtyard.

"Fasho cuz," Tru said throwing up Nahborhood with his hands as his crew did the same.

"Cuz, don't C acting like you the shit now though," Infant Smokey Loc said laughing.

"Cuz, y'all already know this nicca walk around like his shit don't stink when we all know his shitty booty ass do," Blue Shiesty said jokingly making everybody including Tru laugh.

"Cuz, it ain't me that think that. Cuz, it's hoes who can't get enough of the Loc and nicca that's a Tru Blue story," Tru said.

"Dam cuz, I miss my nicca Guuwop crazy ass cuz, I can see cuz jelly that you ain't take him to get inked up too. Y'all know the Bozo would of had a lot to say 'bout this," Minion said as the crew nodded in agreement.

It was time for work since customers were already showing up. Their biweekly re-up was coming soon, so they needed to gather every dollar being put in their hands. They all were starting to really stuff their pockets which resulted in both Blue Shiesty and Infant Smokey Loc getting their own rides, so now everybody in the crew was mobile.

# CHAPTER TWENTY-FIVE

Time was really flying since school had started because before Sasha knew it she was going into her third month of being a high school student. Her birthday had came and long past, now it was October, the month of Halloween which was her third favorite month of the year coming behind her birth month September and December which was Christmas time. She loved to dress up for Halloween, but this year she felt that she was far too old to be trick-or-treating. She was Lady Fierce and she didn't indulge in what was deemed childish behavior. At the least, not openly where it could be seen and criticized because she still secretly loved waking up early on Saturday mornings just to watch all of her favorite cartoons like *Dragon Ball Z* with a big bowl of Fruity Pebbles cereal like she always done since she was a scrawny little girl.

Her big brother had had all of her home girls for the past few weeks talking about him and how good he looked with his NHC neck tattoo which they said made his eyes pop out more. Sasha and Tru had the same colored eyes which they were told came from their great grandfather on their dad's side who had been rumored to be quite the lady's man in his day back in the Dominican Republic. However, their dad and their aunt Marie were the only two out of five kids in total that had colored eyes, but theirs were light brown.

Sasha was chilling with Anna Loc and Karen at Aya Park which had to be no more than one hundred feet from Karen's house. The day had a slight wind chill, so they all had on fashionable windbreakers to keep them warm while they hung up and watched a heated pick up game on the basketball courts. They had been innocently flirting with the ballers who were trying to show out for them in hopes to impress them. Sasha only knew two of the eight dudes playing basketball from school. The others she wasn't sure if they were hood homies or not, but they did have a few who were cute. Anna Loc who was saying she was single and ready to mingle was really making the guys compete for her attention.

"Bitch, yo ass sure acting thirsty," Karen said looking upside Anna Loc's head.

"Bitch, stop hating cuz you see these niccas on me and not you," Anna Loc replied doing her signature head bobble which made her braids sway in the wind.

"Bitch, ain't nobody stunting these niccas. I got me a real nicca," Karen blurted out regretting it the instant it came out.

"Huh? Bitch, let me find out that yo ass been hiding a whole nicca this whole time. Spill it out cuz. Who is he?" Sasha said as her and Anna Loc both looked at Karen with no nonsense faces.

"We ain't really on the boyfriend and girlfriend tip just yet cuz we both ain't trying to get lockdown. It's complicated to say the least. For now I'm gonna keep what we doing between us," Karen said knowing that her home girls weren't going for that.

"Bitch, I know yo nosey ass ain't now trying to keep a secret especially when you C all in our Cs wax," Anna Loc said.

"Yeah bitch, stop avoiding the question. Who yo nicca is?" Sasha asked suspiciously.

"Y'all bitches can't force me to say what I don't want to say right now. I got my reasons cuz I'm not sure if he want our biz out there and like I said we ain't put any labels on what we doing," Karen said getting up from sitting on the park bench where they had been facing the game still being carried on with the participants clearly clueless to the fact that the ladies were no longer watching them try to show out.

"This bitch really ain't gone say shit cuz. I can see in her face that she gone stand on keeping this a secret between her and her boo whatever his name is," Anna Loc said looking from Karen to Sasha.

"Yeah I can see that. Okay sis we will let it go, but for yo sake I just hope he won't hurt you cuz we gone get him for messing over our sis," Sasha said seriously as Anna Loc nodded in agreement.

"Okay I know y'all my sistas for real and always got my cacc," Karen said a little emotional.

"Always," Anna Loc and Sasha both said seriously in unison.

"Jinx," Karen said laughing as she embraced her home girls who laughed with her to lighten the mood some since it had gotten way more serious than they had expected.

"Let's get back to my house cuz it's starting to get a little chiller than it was just thirty minutes ago. Plus, let's leave so these niccas can stop killing themselves for Anna's attention," Karen said adjusting her windbreaker because she felt the chill of the wind creeping through.

Sasha followed her home girls out the park. They waved and said goodbye to the guys who couldn't hide their disappointment that the ladies were leaving them after putting on a speculator showcase of talent and ability like they had been trying impress recruiters from big Division One universities. She stayed stride-for-stride with her home girls who had started talking about something totally different than what they had just finished talking about. However, she still found her mind wondering back to who this mystery guy could be that had her best friend so uptight about simply telling them. She wasn't foolish in the least because she knew that the only reason they breached the subject in the first place was due to a slip up by Karen.

When they got to Karen's house which didn't take long at all, they saw that they were just in time for lunch which reminded them that they were in fact hungry. Karen's mom who Sasha affectionately called Aunt Monica had made them all some arroz con gandules which was a very delicious Puerto Rican rice and beans dish. Consequently, Sasha who was a huge foodie for Caribbean cuisine couldn't wait to sit down and dig in. By the hurried movements of her home girls, she could tell that they felt the same.

# CHAPTER TWENTY-SIX

For the most part October had been real good to Tru and his Crazy Crippin' Crew. They had somehow managed to stay in school while getting their grind on. Nevertheless, their attendance wasn't nowhere near perfect and they were far from being on the honor roll, but they still made sure to show their faces just enough to say to their parents that they were going. Tru still had his sights on a second spot, but now was looking to expand outside the hood because the interior of Park South wasn't showing to be the most lucrative opportunity. He had been back to visit the Townies quite a few times since he first started to see them for what they were which was a million-dollar spot with real takeover potential. Their original spot in the Roesers was still producing steady profits, but due to their limited hours and heavy competition, things had seemed to hit a peak in potential.

However, even though their grind was still looking good, they were still young and very active gang bangers, so they had been finding themselves in various beefs with Opps who were trying to press the line on the Aya. Tru had decided to activate his Crazy Crippin' Crew to ride on the Vistas who had slid through on two different occasions and shot three of the homies putting one in critical condition. This outraged Tru to say the least and now he had murder on his mind and he knew that his crew felt the same especially after hearing all the disses coming from their most hated rivals. At school, some of the homies and home girls had started to get into squabbles with students who banged the Vistas with his sister and her Honeys deep in the mist of it all through their conflicts with the Vista Bloodettes. He always found himself smiling when he thought about how far Sasha had came since he had her properly quoted on to this Nahborhood Crip way of life almost two years ago after she kept begging him that she wanted to be a loc like him. Therefore, he had some home girls jump her in at the hood park which included Anna Loc and his secret boo, Lady Loc. He stayed on the home girls to make sure they made any female representing Park South to know that they would live up to being a member of the Nahborhood because being a coward wouldn't be tolerated at all. Crazy Crippin' was always in full effect.

"Y'all niccas ready to put in work cuz?" Tru said as he got into the front passenger seat of what was to be their murder wagon.

"Cuz, you already know we stay ready," Blue Shiesty replied putting the sawed-off twelve gauge shotgun in his lap as he got ready to mask up with his navy blue rag.

"CC Lit," Infant Smokey Loc said who was to be the driver on this mission even though he wanted to be one of the main shooters.

"CC Lit," Blue Shiesty and Tru said. Minion and Baby Gator had been selected to stay back to run the spot as their crew went to handle this mission because the grind didn't stop for nothing. Money was needed always because it ran the world. In war or peace, no matter what, everything required funding, so some had to get left behind. Nevertheless, they would be credited with the success of this mission as if they hit it because they were a team and every single crew members' hands were grimy with the work they had put in, so nobody was nowhere remotely clean in the least.

They rode down Roeser Road to cross the threshold on Sixteenth Street to enter the part where the Vistas was located. It was completely dark as they went on the hunt for their prey. Tru always got overly excited on these missions and therefore, always had to force himself to sit still instead of slobbering at the mouth like some dog like the Opps he was gunning for tonight. They were somewhat familiar with the layout of their rivals' hood just like their rivals were with theirs which came from years and years of coexisting in open conflict with each other, but this was to be the very first mission of theirs riding through.

"We gone see if we can catch some of these niccas slipping on their main block cuz and make it for real the murder block," Infant Smokey Loc said referring to the nickname Murder Block which was on Thirteenth Street in the Vistas as they entered.

"Fasho cuz," Tru said interlocking his fingers to tighten the black gloves he on as he put his hands back on the Mack Ten he had in his lap.

They all got quiet as they entered the Vistas. The mood got even more tense as they centered their focus to accomplishing the mission. Tru loved the thrill of lurking for a kill which was almost as good as sex in his crazy book of enjoyments. He knew it wasn't normal to find joy in such malice, but he wasn't normal and the world he knew wasn't friendly. Therefore, they stayed dangerous because in his world, there were truly just two things, prey or predator. The fangs and claws he and his crew had clearly showed what they truly were, so they were really just living up to what was their nature. It was as natural to them as a pack of wolves stealthily moving through the woods looking for some unsuspecting deer.

Nonetheless, as they got deeper into their rivals' turf, they found themselves driving by a white Crown Victoria that was clearly gang squad patrolling. This made them tense up even more because this was unexpected to run right into what could be called their most dangerous Opp. The police had a long history of abusing their power in South Phoenix with really no accountability and the gang squad was the most notorious of them all. They had been known to get rid of gangbangers they didn't like through planting things on them, and there were even rumors of a few that had been killed in staged killings to place blame on a rival set. Tru told his homies to keep their composure as they slowly drove by hoping that they wouldn't be of any interest. However, as they got a little farther down the street, they saw that the Crown Victoria was attempting to turn around in an attempt to get behind them and follow.

"Cuz, you already know what to do," Tru yelled as Infant Smokey Loc hit the gas and turned down a side street to get them to one of the few exits the Vistas had which made it a challenge to even dare enter on a mission because it could easily turn against anybody trying to put in work by getting lost behind enemy lines, but Infant Smokey Loc had family in the Vistas and had been through many times as a youth to know about the interior streets.

They find the exit they were looking for on Fourteenth Place and Southern Avenue. Time was of the essence because by now they knew the gang squad officers were most likely trying to play catch up once they saw them floor it to get away. Consequently, Tru felt like his rapidly beating heart were counting down the seconds to the end of his life because he knew that if they got pinned down in any way that he was going to take his chances and start blasting at the cops. They had too much to lose to allow that to happen. His homie was driving like he was a bona fide street racer and getting real little from the scene before more cops showed up to join the chase. They sped through a red light to make a crucial turn on Sixteenth Street and drove northbound in the direction of Roeser Road to get back to their hood where safety lay.

"Dam cuz that was a close call for real," Blue Shiesty said still clutching on to the shotgun in his lap which showed that he had the same thoughts to hold court in the streets instead of getting caught with guns they had on them for the mission which were all dirty from two other missions they had went on that would have linked them to at least one body.

They quickly dropped the car they had rented from a fiend and threw the heats into the trunk of Infant Smokey Loc's car who was going to dump them into a canal far away. Tru knew that tonight was a sign that they better tighten up some more. He was kicking himself mentally in the ass for holding on to guns they had used before because really enjoying the effect they had caused with them wasn't no justification to get away just to potentially get caught with them on another mission gone wrong.

# CHAPTER TWENTY-SEVEN

Looking at herself in the full-length mirror she had on the inside of her closet door, Sasha admired the beautiful young woman looking back at her with her pretty hazel eyes. She swayed her head from side-to-side with some attitude to let her long big single braids that her mom had just finished up earlier shake. Every since she had watched *Poetic Justice*, she had fallen in love with how beautiful Janet Jackson looked throughout the entire movie especially how she had had her hair in the same exact hairstyle Sasha had recreated for her own look today. Her only twist to the look was the navy blue rag she had wrapped around her head because Lady Fierce was due to make her presence known along with some of her fellow Honeys at a party in Hill Top which was her hoods closest and oldest ally. Therefore, it could easily be said that it was like a second hood for her because there wasn't any hostilities between the Aya and the Top. The Honeys had been invited to the party by some of the lady Gangstas they were cool with from there.

The party was set to start at seven o'clock which was still a couple of hours away, so she still had time before she officially finished getting dressed. Her home girl Anna Loc was suppose to be coming to pick her up a little past seven anyways after she first swung by Karen's to pick her up as well. They were going to purposely show up a little late at least ten deep to make an entrance which was what they were known to do because the Nahborhood Honeys were showstoppers and head turners wherever they went.

She couldn't believe that October was almost over. Halloween was going to be next Saturday, and Sasha along with her Honeys had been putting together a Nahborhood costume block party that she couldn't wait to throw on Karen's home block of Carver Drive. Her big brother who was looking like a real Nahborhood celebrity was going to be performing a couple of songs at Aya Park that he and two of his Crazy Crippin' homies had recorded recently. As her bro and his crew loved to say, it was going to be CC Lit for sure.

"Hey Sassy, you look so beautiful hija," Sabrina said admiring her daughter from the bedroom door.

"Hey mamí, thank you. You know I get my looks from you," Sasha said as she looked at the gorgeous woman standing before her.

"Those braids does look good on you. At first, I was skeptical about them even though we know whatever I do always comes out super dope and clean. But I never did them like that big before. It does give you that back in the 'Nineties feel," Sabrina said smiling.

"Yeah I love them mom and I can't wait to shock all my home girls tonight when I step out. I know that they are going to be jealous fasho," Sasha said.

"I know they are because my baby girl is a looker. You just be safe out there okay. I want you and Karen to be here no later than one o'clock okay," Sabrina said stepping up to embrace her daughter in a tight hug with a kiss on her forehead.

Around a quarter till seven, Sasha finished up getting dressed. She had put on her blue Troy Aikeman's Dallas Cowboy Jersey because they were her favorite them, some tight blue jeans, and for her shoes, she had opted to wear her blue and white Nike Dopemans which went with the 'Nineties vibe she was portraying. She couldn't wait to stop people in their tracks as they got a look at the always beautiful infamous Lady Fierce. Niggas left-and-right were always vying for her attention, but none of them could measure up to her standards.

"Cuz, you sure ain't say you was going to show up looking like one of the female Original Crips," Anna Loc said as she run up to hug her home girl.

"Yeah you sure kept this to yourself cuz," Karen said smiling as she got her hug in to.

"It's called a surprise and y'all bitches are jealous cuz y'all know I'm the only one who could pull this off," Sasha said jokingly as she showed off her new look.

"Bitch you know I look good in just about anything," Anna Loc said.

"Y'all bitches know dam well I'm the one who is the one most fashioned forward," Karen said which was the truth because Karen had an eye for fashion and trends that none of them had and had many times before put together a look for all the Honeys to wear. A big reason why their clique stood out wasn't just because of their reputation to fight, it was how stylized they were and their swag that really got them all the way up there. Even their rivals the Southern Belles and Vista Bloodettes occasionally acknowledged that Honeys did know how to dress to impress when they all weren't trying to pull each others' hair out.

"Yeah bitch for the most part you are fasho our fashion designer which I keep saying you should really consider as yo calling cuz you are so passionate about it," Sasha said putting on a jacket because it was a little cold outside.

"And I've been thinking about it too cuz you are right," Karen said as they left back out Sasha's house to get in Anna Loc's car.

The drive to Hill Top didn't take them that long at all as they crossed Sixteenth Street and Baseline Road to head into the South Mountain area. Before leaving the hood, however, they had met up with two other cars that carried the other Honeys who were going to accompany them up to the party. Consequently, just like it had been with Karen and Anna Loc, Sasha's other Honey home girls had been jealous that she didn't give them a heads up about the retro look for tonight, so they too could have all coordinated like they always did on their group look. However, Sasha honestly wanted her own individuality for tonight. She couldn't tell her home girls any of this because they would be hurt, but she wanted to standout even amongst them and be viewed as just Lady Fierce.

By the time they got to the party, it was already in full effect with activity which was how they wanted it to be. They had to park around the corner on the next street over, however, because the street was filled with cars of residents and the few leftover spaces in between had already been filled with other party goers' cars. Sasha and her eleven Honeys walked up to the house where the party was being thrown at and made every eye around watch them as they entered the front door once their Hill Top home girl Trisha saw that they had arrived.

The party was packed and got even more packed once they filtered in throughout the available areas which included the backyard. Sasha, Karen, and Anna Loc all stayed together for the most part being the shot callers for their clique until Anna Loc was escorted away by her on-again-off-again boyfriend, Moony Loc who had clearly been waiting for her arrival. They ended up finding a spot on the wall where they immediately started to grind on each other to the music playing. This left Sasha and Karen together who were just enjoying each others' company not caring about any of the niggas who kept trying to get them to dance with them. Sasha was content to dance with her home girls until she was approached by the most handsome stranger that she had ever seen with a beautiful smile. To her displeasure, however, she could tell he was most likely from an Opp hood with all the red he had on. Nonetheless, she felt drawn to him for some odd reason she couldn't explain, but she wanted to make sure she didn't let him know the effect he was already having on her.

"Hey beautiful, I know you hear that all the time, but I couldn't help it. I have been watching you from just across the way turn down guy after guy and almost didn't take my chance," Knerdie B said as they were now dancing into a third song.

"Well I almost dismissed you too, but I liked yo approach which wasn't too thirsty," Sasha said as she couldn't hold back the smile that appeared on her face looking up into his handsome dark chocolate face with his piercing dark brown eyes.

"Oh so I did have some thirst involved huh?" Knerdie B said laughing.

"Yeah a lil bit of thirst is cool," Sasha said as she followed him into the backyard where they could talk without having to yell over the music.

"So I finally get to meet the notorious Lady Fierce. I can say without a doubt that you are fiercely beautiful fasho," Knerdie B said.

"The one and only. I see you know about me but I don't know about you. I see you and yo boys in all that red, so I assume y'all some Bloods. I don't normally deal with y'all at all honestly cuz my bro would trip if he saw me talking to you. Shit you saw some of the looks we already got from my home girls tonight," Sasha said.

"Well I like a good Romeo and Juliet hood story," Knerdie B said as he looked into her pretty cat eyes that held him in her gaze, "But me and my Boyz are from the Front Streets and yes, I know you are from Park South. I don't care because I felt the need to introduce myself and I'm glad I did."

"Okay, I like yo attitude Mr. Knerdie B and yo unique name cuz I ain't never met anybody by that C fore," Sasha said knowing deep down she was very happy that he had taken the chance and broke the ice between them because she would have never dared to talk to him in any way otherwise.

They spent the next hour or so just talking away getting to know each other a little better. Their conversation was so good that either allowed for any interruption. This included not allowing either one of his Boyz or her Honeys to pull them away from each other. Sasha found out that he was a freshman like her at South and that she did know about him from hearing about his skills on the basketball courts. It was just something about Knerdie B that made her want to throw all caution to the wind and further get to know him regardless of the backlash she knew was coming from both her brother and her home girls. It was her decision and she would deal with any hard time they gave her about it.

# Lady Hood Square

# CHAPTER TWENTY-EIGHT

## 2022

The year had been going by so well for them that Sasha Bukhari considered it to be their most productive one yet. She was in the final steps of finally becoming a board certified psychologist and was thinking about possibly going the extra mile to become a board certified psychiatrist. Nevertheless, she was finally about to be able to put doctor in front of her name because Dr. Bukhari did have a nice ring to it. After getting her Bachelor of Applied Arts and Science from the esteemed Howard University back in 2017, she hadn't wasted no time in applying to the School Psychology (PH.D) Howard University Arts and Science to get accepted into their accelerated Doctor of Psychology graduate studies program. Now she had successfully gotten her Doctor of Psychology (PsyD) degree and had more than the required four thousand hours of supervised experience through internships at Washington Hospital and her current job at Howard University Hospital in Washington, DC where she spent a lot of her time nowadays. The step she had left was to take the Examination for Professional Practice in Psychology to become eligible to apply for her license in DC.

After having their second child in 2018, Sasha and her husband Kamal Bukhari had decided to move out of their Northwest Washington, DC apartment to the small town of Mitchellville in Prince George's County, Maryland which was an upper-middle-class African American community where black people made up over eighty-five percent of the population and had a median household income over one hundred thousand dollars. It was ranked fourth in the nation on the Ten Most Affluent African American Communities list. It was a perfect location for them to raise a family while still being able to travel back into DC for work because it was only thirty minutes away. Therefore, she was able to take the drive daily with her two kids who were both attending Howard University Early Learning Program which was a preschool program and daycare facility very close to her job. Her daughter Khadija was five years old and her son Samir was four years old. They were the apples of her eyes. Khadija looked like a mini female version of her father with her darker complexion and dimples while Samir resembled her with his hazel eyes and lighter skin.

The year was coming to an end soon which meant it was almost time for her husband's birthday which was December twelfth. He was going to be turning twenty-eight years old, and just like her twenty-eighth birthday back on September eighth, they were going to really celebrate life together and the blessings that Allah has been bestowing on them because they had been blessed even though at times they had to work together on overcoming life struggles. They were constantly reminded that with hardship comes ease and as long as they had each other, there wasn't no task too difficult for them to handle. This was something she always admired about her husband, his willingness to be a team player and not try to dominate her as his wife like most tended to think because they were traditional in their Islamic beliefs with her priding herself on wearing her hijab whenever she left the house.

"As Salamu Alaikum," Sasha said as she greeted her husband at the door.

"Wa Alaikum as Salam. Hey Sunshine," Kamal replied as he kissed his wife briefly.

"Hey my Love. I've missed you today. We had a rare half day today at the hospital because I had been prepping for the EPPP test next Tuesday in'sha Allah," Sasha said.

"Oh okay my Love. I know you are going to pass with flowing colors because you have been going harder in paint than Shaq in his heyday," Kamal said as he put his things down and walked with her to the dining room table where he gladly saw that dinner was ready to be served because he was starving after a long day of activities with the inner-city kids who were a part of his at risk youth program in DC. His nonprofit organization named after his brand Hood Square operated primarily in DC, but he had aspirations of expanding throughout the whole DMV which had some very tough youths all over. He loved what he did for a living and was glad he could focus more on giving back to the communities that raised kids who most gave up on simply because they didn't care to take the time to get to know that behind the hard shell was a kid like any other kid, who wanted to be loved. The clothing line that had started it all was doing real good with his dear homie and partner Jonny back on the West Coast running the daily operations. They were now in most of the major clothing stores in the country and had an even stronger online presence through working with Amazon.

"You and all these basketball references. I know those kids be loving how you be coaching them too on the fundamentals. The development league you had launched this summer had been amazing to watch because you do have some very talented kids on the roster," Sasha said referring the summer basketball league he had started over the past summer that had been an instant hit throughout DC which had gained the support of some very influential people in the DMV who wanted in on helping more kids. The league had given a lot of these kids the opportunity to showcase themselves in front of audiences who most likely would have never seen them play due to the rough sections of the city they lived in. She was so proud that they had never forgotten their South Phoenix roots that made them into the highly intelligent, very ambitious individuals they were today because being both Streetwise and Booksmart had given them a sharper edge which made a Hood Square stand out from the rest.

"Yeah, you know my love affair with the game ain't never ceased. I love this as a way to bond with the kids who normally give you the coldest shoulders you would ever feel," Kamal said with a smile because he had had some real breakthroughs with a few of his toughest kids who were repeat offenders with the juvenile system in DC metropolitan area.

"Yeah, I can't wait to be able to be fully licensed to be able to really start putting all my years of education and working in the psychology field to use in giving back to our community," Sasha said as she served her husband his bowl of Pollo guisado.

"Yes I know mi amor. I'm so proud of you Wifey. Where are my babies?" Kamal said as he started to eat the delicious Dominican dish of braised chicken.

"Their bad butts are in their rooms resting after long day of trying to wear me out. They were happy after I came to get them a little early because my studies hadn't went as long as expected. We had spent time going to Stead Park before we came home around five o'clock," Sasha said.

"I bet they were a handful. They get all that energy from their beautiful mother," Kamal said looking at his beautiful wife who was so full of youthful energy that fueled him in times where he wanted to quit, but being his backbone, she forbid him from ever giving up on his purpose in life which is why he had come so far since getting out of the Arizona Department of Corrections back in 2016 after doing a five year bid. He had never looked back and had decided to make living in DC permanent after falling in love with its strong black culture. For the most part, the city had welcomed Knerdie B aka Tha Real Hood Square with open arms and had been infatuated with his Hood Square brand. He had even transferred to Howard University for his graduate studies after finally getting his Bachelors of Arts in Communication Studies with Ashland University which started while he was still in prison.

"Yeah, don't act like I don't be knowing you be putting them up to trying to run circles around me. I'm going to for sure get you back when they come to work with you over the break in December because I'm going to sit around the house and kick my feet up. During that time I will be taking some time to myself from my mommy and work duties. I'm going to let my handsome strong husband pamper me like he always does and yes I'm looking to get my feet rubbed every single day you bring our little brats back," Sasha said sitting across the table from him nibbling on her food because she wasn't that hungry.

"Baby you already know I'm down to rub whatever you want me to," Kamal said looking at her knowingly which made her blush.

"Hubby, you already know the kids are going to be out for the count, so yes I want you to give me those special massages I love so much," Sasha said looking at her husband who locked eyes with her which made her tremble with anticipation.

Consequently, he quickly finished up the last few morsels on his plate and got up to escort her to their upstairs bedroom because their house was a two-story with five bedrooms, three bathrooms, a large living room, spacious kitchen, and had the biggest backyard they ever had. It had a pool that they had fenced in due to them having two very young kids who loved to explore. They had just recently gotten a beautiful male Staffordshire bull terrier puppy who was only six months old to raise with the kids for companionship and also have as a guard dog because the breed was well-known to be very protective of their families.

---

# CHAPTER TWENTY-NINE

It was good day to pull up on some of the kids in his outreach program in the Benning Ridge neighborhood in Southeast DC which was considered to be one of the most dangerous areas in the city. He had taken the advice of his O' G homie and big Muslim brother Trevor Green Jr. aka Lil Tre Way who was doing so good back in South Phoenix after getting paroled from walking off twenty-five straight years in prison. He was both a mentor and inspiration to Kamal who had always looked up to him and found sound advice every time. It had been a blessing to be able to be at a point to give his O' G homie a job as one of the first full-time mentors for Tha Hood Square Movement fresh out of prison and then to see him vastly improve their reach-one-teach-one mentorship program out in Arizona to a point that they had expanded into West Phoenix and Tucson. Trevor was helping him refine the techniques he was employing in DC by working more closely with the guys who were some of the most respected in their hoods to obtain that sway with their younger homies. This gave him the credibility he needed to make these teenagers more open to talk to him being that he wasn't from their hoods. He had also started implementing Trevor's strategy of using sports as a way to bridge gaps with these inner-city youths, but instead of boxing like Trevor was doing in Arizona, Kamal had started to use basketball because he had grew up playing it almost every single day. He had been one of the best high school basketball players in Phoenix prior to getting incarcerated at the age of sixteen. He had had big dreams of one day going pro and playing in the NBA as a superstar point guard.

However, things had happened and life for him had went a different route which in his opinion was all for the better because he had a life that he couldn't complain about. He had the most beautiful wife who was his best friend and biggest supporter with two beautiful rapidly growing kids, and he had successfully launched Hood Square to the world at large. The brand had taken off faster than he had expected which had made him recruit his very business savvy homie Jonny to partner up with him to be the Square to his Hood. Now their urban clothing line had three different versions which was the signature line Hood Square, the female line Lady Hood Square dedicated to his wife who had her best friend Karen as the lead clothing designer, and Hood Square Jr. which was the kids line they had successfully introduced to the world over two years ago.

Nonetheless, he had found out that coaching was a lot more difficult than he expected which made him contact his old coach from high school for some essential tips on how to work with teens who were hardened by the environments they came up in. Coach Blackwell had been more than pleased to aid and assist. Consequently, this new strategy took off so fast it gave him the opportunity to create a small summer league and start recruiting some of the same guys who had helped him get access to some of these tough areas as volunteer league coaches and officials to officiate the games. In their first season over the past summer, they had six teams who were from the various hoods throughout DC and that number was bound to grow by the time the next season started. It wasn't the We Got Next just yet which was an elite summer league in Arizona that played teams from other summer leagues throughout the West Coast region, but with time, more development, and an increase in popularity, it could become the DMV urban version. He was currently brainstorming an official name for the league to make it more legitimate because every organized league had one.

When he had first moved to the city, he had thought that he would never get adjusted to how cold it got in DC, but he had quickly learned early on how to bundle up like the locals. Kamal saw the cold weather as an opportunity to showcase his fashion and rock some of the brand's winter gear like their new bomber jackets with the big Hood Square logo on the back with Streetwise going down the front right side of the jacket and Booksmart on the opposite left side. The jackets had become a big hit in DC and was being sported in social media post throughout the Eastern Seaboard. It wasn't winter in DC yet, but he could feel the cold getting ready to settle in. He was glad that the day's temperatures had allowed him to step out wearing a simple red Hood Square t-shirt and Hood Square blue jeans. His team back at the Arizona headquarters had yet to figure out a potential style for the Hood Square sneakers they wanted to eventually add to their line, so he had put on some red, white, and blue Nike Air Maxes because he loved the feel of walking on a cloud from the bubble soles that made them such a popular pair of sneakers to wear. His wardrobe wasn't complete without the red kufi he wore on his head because he literally had dozens of them in various colors to match any outfit he put on.

"Knerdie B, my main man one hundred grand, it's sure is good to see you back in the hood because the South Side missed you," Spade said who was one of the most respected niggas to come out of the Benning Terrace Apartments aka the notorious Simple City. He was one of the first people to embrace Kamal as a homie when he first moved to DC in 2017. Spade who was five years older than Kamal unfortunately like so many other similarly situated people had a criminal history. He had walked off a ninety-six month sentence in the Bureau of Prisons where he spent most of his time on high level United States Penitentiary yards like USP - Leavenworth in Leavenworth, Kansas and USP - Marion in Marion, Illinois. During his time inside, Spade had become a high ranking member of a prison organization called the DC Blacks which led to him extending his sentence due to the work he had to put in to climb the ranks. Nevertheless, he had gotten out in 2016 and with some assistance from Kamal, had successfully transitioned back into society as a pillar of his community and was no longer the menace society had branded him to be. He had recently become an official mentor on the payroll to help Kamal's DC youth outreach mentorship program for his nonprofit, Tha Hood Square Movement.

"What's good with my moe? You know I'm a South Side baby also, so I go to it no matter what area code I'm in," Kamal said happily as he walked the short distance from his 2020 all black Chevrolet Trailblazer which had become his work car to shake hands with Spade and embrace him in front of the spot he had been chilling at.

Kamal didn't micromanage his mentors which were six in total spread throughout DC in some of its toughest hoods because he trusted them wholeheartedly to do the task at hand. He had recently selected the most trustworthy of the his volunteers to become official mentors. The mentorship program had already been implemented in South Phoenix. He had finally decided to bring it out to DC as well due to the success of the pilot program with Trevor at the helm. However, the mentorship program was still in its beginning stages, so they all were learning as they went to help develop the best program for each particular hood they operated in. Kamal helped out with the kids who were interested in playing basketball for the summer league while his mentors were responsible for the day-to-day activities for all the kids in the program because he couldn't be in every single spot all the time especially with his rapidly increasing Executive Director responsibilities for the entire nonprofit which included the operations on the West Coast. He normally spent a lot of his time nowadays at the Hood Square East Coast headquarters located in Northeast DC which had become the exclusive home for the nonprofit subsidiary of Hood Square while the much larger headquarters in Arizona oversaw the entire for-profit business part of his organization with his partner Jonny as the Chief Operations Officer because he was still the CEO. Kamal had plans to move the DC headquarters to a bigger location in Bowie, Maryland because he was also working on a potential partnership with Bowie State University which was a public HBCU in Prince George's County not that far from where he lived. If this deal went through, Tha Hood Square Movement would be expanding into parts of Central and Southern Maryland where its outreach efforts were most needed.

"Moe, you know you should have given me a bigger heads up before you came, but the lil moes gone be siced to see you once they get out of school. I've been taking some classes on how to be a tutor, so I can start being more hands on to help them keep their grades up because my lil moes Yeti and G Boy have been loafin' a lot at school lately and not taking their education seriously like I've been telling them. I keep warning them that if they keep on with this behavior that they will be going to the School of Hard Knocks for real where they are going to be severely tested and tested over and over and we both know in those situations, the consequences ain't no joke for those who can't pass the test," Spade said as they walked to through the grounds to hang out for a bit and catch up while they waited for the kids they were mentoring who were known as Junior Hood Squares.

"I'm excited to see them as well because it's been a minute since I've been able to come to this part of town with the heavy workload at headquarters. And fasho stay on the lil homies because if we can help it, I don't want them ever having to do time especially as a juvenile like we unfortunately had to endure with these Hard Knock rules we learned to live by while on the inside. Oh yeah, next week don't forget about the board meeting because I want all my DC mentors to be there too, so y'all can add y'all input on things we can do to improve our mission. I started this nonprofit because Hood Square is a movement and a way of life to help people like us avoid the traps that society have set for us and free the ones who have fell into them. We still have a tall task ahead of us in DC alone, but we have made some very impressive gains over these last few months for real. In'sha Allah, I'm thinking about implementing the mentorship program in Baltimore now that we are close to relocating the headquarters to Maryland," Kamal said.

"Moe, you already know some of the moes gone feel like you siding with some bamas when they hear about you going to B More, but off that because I would be wellin' if I told you otherwise, because I'm so proud to be a part of this movement and will be honored to offer any assistance in making it better suited for the communities it was designed for. You already know that you can't go anywhere in DC nowadays without seeing somebody wearing a Hood Square something. You know my favorites are the hoodies because they go with absolutely everything I wear and can keep me warm even in some of the coldest winter moments," Spade said.

"It has been an honor knowing you bro. Since day one, you have welcomed me with opened arms and had opened doors for the movement to grow out here that may not have opened otherwise. I'm happy to have you now officially on the team. We are going to continue to keep going up from here in'sha Allah. How have things been out this way?" Kamal said remembering the ongoing war between Simple City and their bitter rivals Thirty-seventh Street who were just five minutes away.

"Moe, you know shit ain't simple in Simple City, but we maintain and keep going," Spade said.

"Yeah, I feel you on that bro because it's like that where I'm from as well," Kamal said referring to the very complicated relationship his hood had with his wife's hood.

Nonetheless, it didn't take long for word to get out that he was in Simple City through the power of social media which made more people show up to meet and greet him. Kamal better known as Knerdie B aka Tha Real Hood Square had become somewhat of a celebrity over these last few years since officially launching his brand back in 2016. He was a man that wore many hats nowadays as an entrepreneur, author even though he had yet to write another book other than the one he had written for his wife while incarcerated which had become a national bestseller, mentor to both the urban youth and formerly incarcerated which led to him becoming a well sought after motivational speaker, and he was considering to finally start Tha Real Hood Square Podcast. His wife Sasha too had become very popular because of her Lady Hood Square persona which she had fully embraced and made come to life over these years. He knew she really liked being a role model for girls of color because she represented so many things as an educated Afro Latina woman who was a proud Muslima and a mother. He was so proud to see her about to catch her dreams of becoming a licensed psychologist who could easily practice anywhere she wanted to, so he was honored to have her wanting to come on full time to run Tha Hood Square Movement with him. She planned to develop a Lady Hood Square mentor program specifically designed to address the special needs of girls and women from the inner-cities and urban suburbs.

---

# CHAPTER THIRTY

October tenth had finally arrived which was the day she had been prepping for since the day of her graduation, so she was getting ready to head out to the Pearson Professional Center in Northeast DC to take her Examination for Professional Practice in Psychology. This was the last step she needed to take before she could achieve the goal she had set for herself during her first year at Howard University. She also planned to become certified in Maryland in the beginning of next year since it was the state that she resided in and where their headquarters was relocating. However, she would have to take the additional Maryland Jurisprudence Exam before she got license which covered the state's Code of Ethics and Professional Conduct and other state-specific regulations and laws pertaining to the practice of psychology.

Sasha heard her phone ringing as she was finishing up getting dressed and making sure she had everything she would need for the day because she would be going into work following the exam. She was home alone because her husband had taken the kids with him on his way to work to allow her the time needed to focus just on the task at hand. The love and support he constantly gave her were two of the many things that kept her falling deeper and deeper in love with him throughout these years. He jokingly told her the love pit he pushed her in was truly bottomless and she believed him because she had yet to feel like she was getting close to any type of surface. She rushed back into her bedroom where she had left her phone which was the new iPhone fourteen because they were a couple that loved everything from Apple which included the iPads she got for the kids and the iMac Pros that could be found in every office at their headquarters including the one they shared at home. Sasha's face immediately lit up as soon as she saw who it was trying to FaceTime with her.

"Hey sis," Sasha said as soon as she answered and saw her best friend/sister-in-law's beautiful face looking back at her.

"Hey sis, you know I wasn't going miss the opportunity to wish you luck, but we both know you don't need it cuz you got this," Karen said.

"Aww, thank you sis because you know I appreciate you. Yeah, I know I'm ready, but I'm still a little nervous because all my years of schooling and staying discipline are about to be summed up in this two-part exam I have to answer with a passing score of point-five," Sasha said feeling like her nerves were trying to get the best of her.

"You cut that out girl cuz like I said, you know you got this. Like you said all them years of going to school and staying disciplined are about to be summed up in this moment and they are going to show true like the blue you got on," Karen said smiling.

"Yeah, I know you right. You know I still can't get me enough of my true blue no matter what. Speaking of true blue, where is your husband at? He probably still sleeping huh?" Sasha said.

"Girl, yeah he still sleeping cuz we had a long night," Karen said giggling. "And that's exactly why you pregnant right now for the third time since bro been out. What, it's only been like two years now right? And since then, y'all can't keep y'all hands off each other. My nephew Lil Santi gone have three little siblings now," Sasha said giggling as well.

"Girl, like your husband is to you, mine is my papí for real. Yes I can't get enough of his sexy-eyed Dominican ass with his long dreads and tattoos everywhere. He came home to me on hub and horny, so what could you expect," Karen said laughing some more.

Laughing almost uncontrollably, Sasha barely replied, "Y'all just nasty."

"And like y'all, we are proud of it. But Tru still doing good. He been working with Trevor on improving the mentorship out here. It seems like every kid from the South Side wants to be a Junior Hood Square now. The program has really taken off since reputable niccas from almost every hood have signed up to be a part of Tha Hood Square Movement," Karen said.

"Yeah I know. Kamal is now out here trying to emulate what is going on in AZ. And he is starting to really make an impact out here with the youth and community at large especially ever since he started that basketball league over the summer which gained some serious attention from the powers that be in DC," Sasha said wrapping her long jet-black hair up in a bun so she could put on her navy blue hijab. "That headscarf really do bring out your pretty eyes sis and I see you rocking one of the new Lady Hood Square sweaters I designed. We set release them in December for our 2022-2023 winter line," Karen said with pride who had become the creative force behind Lady Hood Square ever since Sasha got her to come on and use her cold sense of fashion and passion for clothing design. Karen had been somewhat of their stylist during their teenage days in South Phoenix as the infamous Nahborhood Honeys. They had been head tuners and the center of attention wherever they went. Sasha had encouraged her best friend to go to the Arizona State University School of Arts where she got a Bachelor in Fashion to refine her skills way before Lady Hood Square was even a thing, so when her husband had decided he wanted to launch it, it made perfect sense to hire Karen on to develop the style that made it such a hit with girls and women all over even those who wasn't hood at all because the urban chic vibe of Lady Hood Square could be worn on almost any occasion.

"Aww, girl thank you because you know I got my fashion forward sense from you. Yeah, two days ago I got a small shipment of some of your latest designs from Jonny to look over and I love every single piece which is why I had to start wearing them. People expect me to live up to being Lady Hood Square the wife of Tha Real Hood Square himself, so I keep my look all the way up and can't get caught without having something of the brand on," Sasha said seriously as she was heading out of the door.

"Okay sis, I'm glad you like them. I see you heading out, so I'm going to talk to you later okay. Drive safe, I love you," Karen said.

"Okay sis, I love you too and let your Hubby know I'm proud of him," Sasha said as she placed her phone into the windshield mount and put her key in the ignition to rev it up. She had a 2023 blue Kia Sorento that she had got as a birthday gift from her very thoughtful husband. She immediately put on *"Cuff It"* by her favorite artist of all time Beyoncé and started the thirty plus minute drive towards DC to go take the real final exam that would determine if she was really cut out to be a licensed psychologist or not. Nonetheless, she felt her confidence boost as she vibe out and let her mind not wonder about anything but conquering another test like she always did with flying colors. She had managed to keep her GPA at a three-point-nine throughout her entire college career and was also proud of her husband for enrolling in the master's program at Howard University where he eventually received his MBA back 2020.

CHAPTER THIRTY-ONE

---

Another blessed Friday had come around for Kamal which could easily be said was his favorite day of the week. It was very important to his Islamic way of life for sure because it was the day Juma'ah services were held which was Friday Congregational Prayer. Since getting back right with his Islamic way of life while he was in prison, he made sure to fulfill his religious obligation of attending these services which were held noon time every Friday. The Islamic Center of Washington, DC had become his home mosque since becoming a resident in the DMV region. The DC mosque reminded him of the Islamic Community Center of Tempe back in his home state of Arizona which had sent the Imam who had officiated his prison wedding to the love of his life, so it held a special place in his heart.

Therefore, looking at the time, Kamal started getting ready to leave his office for the day to head to Northwest DC aka Uptown where the Islamic Center of Washington DC was located. As was the usual case, he had had a very busy morning filled with meeting after meeting with both his staff in DC and in Arizona. His partner Jonny had been filling him in on the status of where they were at with getting things ready for the upcoming launch of the newest things to come from Hood Square which included all three of the clothing lines. He was excited about introducing the world to the hottest trends that his urban brand was creating.

Also, he had somehow fit in a thirty minute video visit with his best Gangsta homie, Ticko Loon the Goon who was still incarcerated in the Arizona Department of Corrections Rehabilitation and Reentry. His childhood homie was walking off the last few years of a sixteen year sentence. It was always good to see all of his closet homies who were more like his brothers, but nowadays with work and family life, it didn't happen as often as he would like. Nevertheless, when they did find time, they always made the best of it. He was planning to go back to Arizona in the beginning of next year for a week to be able to spend some time with his Boyz. Brazy and Outlaw were still going hard with their music which kept them very busy. They had recently wrapped up a three month long international tour that took them all over Europe and Africa. Lil S Dogg had thankfully retired from being a terror in the streets and had surprisingly turned into one of his most influential mentors.

Leaving Juma'ah services, Kamal went back to Northeast DC which was the largest section of DC to visit one of his mentors. Slim Trigga who proudly represented his hood, Trinidad, had become a good homie of his ever since meeting him over a year ago at a Black Lives Matter rally on Capitol Hill. Kamal had instantly clicked with Slim Trigga after sharing their views of the injustices going on in this country. They had kept in touch mainly through social media where they continued to build with each other. It hadn't taken much thought when Kamal had decided to offer him a job as a mentor. Slim Trigga had felt honored for the opportunity to do his part in uplifting the youth of Northeast. He was already a very vocal advocate for issues concerning Northeast communities who were predominantly African American. One of his biggest issues concerning his hood and beyond was the gentrification going on throughout the Northeast which was displacing the black community. He saw the horrors of gentrification which had rich developers coming into the hood to buy up lots of property for dirt cheap just to raise the rent to impossible rates. Consequently, this tactic forced many black residents to move which gave the developers the opportunity to tear down the old structures to replace them with very expensive new ones. This ensured that the old inhabitants couldn't afford to move back into the areas they had grown up in creating space for more well off occupants who were most likely white. This was happening all over the country though, so it wasn't uniquely a DC problem. Nonetheless, it was a problem that needed to be resolved because it was causing too many impoverished black and brown citizens to get booted out of their homes. Many low income families were now seeing their old neighborhoods getting devoured like carcasses by developers with vulture-like mentalities.

Therefore, Kamal was planning to use his growing influence inside DC to gain an audience with the mayor and other black politicians to make the voices of the hood heard loud and clear because there was too many issues plaguing the black community throughout the Nation's Capital. The numbers backed this up completely because DC was number six in youth incarceration and number two in youth homelessness. It was also in the top ten of homicides in the country every year. As he got deeper into his mission of uplifting the hoods of America, he was learning more effective ways to really give back from the guys he was employing as mentors and from the many more who were joining on as volunteers. This is why he planned to get with Trevor on what they could possibly do to address the gentrification problem that had been going on in South Phoenix for the better part of a decade which had lead to so many being moved to areas like Laveen which was now considered as an extension of the South Side with so many South Phoenix residents now living in the once rural looking community that neighbored South Phoenix, and suburban cities in the West Valley like Tolleson.

"The original Slim Trigga, what's good my nigga," Kamal said happily as he shook hands and embraced his good homie who had been waiting on him to pull up.

"Aye slim, you already know you my moe fasho. Wait till we go get the lil moes cuz they gone be trippin' like big shoes to see you Knerdie B. It's been a hot second since we seen you on the Northeast even though headquarters is on this side of town," Slim Trigga said as they walked through his hood.

"I know, I know, but I've been liking the progress reports you been giving me at our meetings of the minds and you already know I greatly appreciated your input at the first board meeting I had y'all attend. You really did impress. You're very articulate in how you express your values my nigga fasho. I plan to have you and Spade accompany me when I do get this meeting with the mayor next month in'sha Allah," Kamal said.

"I would be honored slim. Growing up in the Northeast, I never thought one day I would be living my life with so much purpose and able to really help out the hood I love so dear. Mugs thought I was lunchin' when I first started down this path cuz they were like shit ain't gone ever change. But we are showing that we can impact the type of change we need if we work together slim cuz collectively we are a force to be reckoned with," Slim Trigga said passionately as they went to where some the his little homies hung out that he had recruited as Junior Hood Squares.

"What up big moe?" Boogey Slim said excitingly when he saw them walking up. He was a tall sixteen year old who looked to be in his early twenties with his full beard and seasoned vibe which growing up in tough urban environments had a way of doing to the youth through exposing them to things that their eyes should never see. Kamal really liked young Boogey Slim and knew he played an important part in getting his homies to take being a part of the mentorship program seriously, but Kamal also knew that they couldn't expect for their Junior Hood Squares to be living like saints and change their ways overnight because that wasn't realistic at all, so he allowed his mentors to work patiently with their chosen juniors and determine who would continue to receive mentoring. As a result of Boogey Slim's outburst, the rest of the group of five teenagers took notice of their big homie walking up with Tha Real Hood Square. They immediately rushed to them to properly greet them. Kamal couldn't help but smile every time he got to hang out with the youth because when they took a liken to somebody they made sure that it was known. He knew if they wasn't feeling a person, that they had absolutely no problem in giving the coldest of shoulders. This was the case no matter if he was in DC, back in South Phoenix, or any hood in America because a person had to demonstrate sincerity if they really wanted to build a rapport with these hardened teens.

"Knerdie B, you been really making sure we ain't looking like some bum joints with all this Hood Square gear you been giving us and our families slim," Nitty Slim said who was a short dark skinned fifteen year old that was outspoken and would give somebody a piece of his mind no matter if it wasn't going to be well received. Therefore, he had also developed a fierce reputation as a fighter. He had recently gotten out of the Youth Services Center after doing eight months when he was originally only was suppose to do five months because of fighting and property damage from a sprinkler he had popped. Now back out, he had been selected by his big homie for mentorship because he was exactly the type of youth the mentorship program was developed to help.

"That's just a small token of appreciation for y'all coming a long way in such a short period of time. I know coming from where y'all come from, shit ain't never been sweet, so whatever we can do to help out, we will. Y'all mentor has been telling me about y'all spreading the word to other homies y'all know to help bring more who need our help to the movement," Kamal said to the entire group who were listening attentively to his every word.

"And y'all lil moes make sure y'all ain't having me wellin' on y'all behalf," Slim Trigga said laughingly which made them laugh as well.

"Big Slim, you know we ain't never made you look bad cuz we believe in what y'all doing," Boogey Slim said on the behalf of his homies who all nodded in agreement.

"That means a lot cuz y'all my lil moes and I just really want the best for y'all cuz y'all are the future of Trinidad and DC as a whole. We gotta strengthen y'all for the fight ahead cuz these mugs are going all in to strip us of our identities again like they stole it from our ancestors by kidnapping them and enslaving them in this country. Now they simply hate us for our resilience and are displacing us instead of giving us the aid we so much deserve from being deprived for so long, but we ain't going to just sit back and let them think they can hoodwink us and steal our hood right from under our noses," Slim Trigga said filled with passion and righteous anger.

"We ain't no rolla crew and ain't gone let nobody treat us like no bamas. We got you," Nitty Slim said.

They were very excited when Kamal told them that he was taking them all to the world famous Ben's Chili Bowl for dinner. His wife had originally put him on to the black owned restaurant when they lived in Uptown. He had been pleased to find out that they also had a Northeast location not too far from his headquarters. The original chili half smokes and the bowl of the famous chili con carne were absolutely mouthwatering good, but it was Virginia's Favorite Banana Pudding that kept bringing him back. It was so good that he even bought the eight-pack often to take home for him and his family to enjoy.

# CHAPTER THIRTY-TWO

They had decided to take a full family day for their rare day off. Saturday was considered the weekend, but in reality for them, the week was a continuous loop like the diamond encrusted platinum infinity necklace Kamal had bought Sasha years ago as an anniversary gift. She knew that the kids deserved a day out with both of their parents being attentive to them with no distractions, so the full focus would be on having fun. Her babies were growing so fast. They never ceased to amaze her on just how intelligent and perceptive they were at only five and four years old. She could hold a decent conversation with both and never had to guess what each wanted because they never had a problem expressing when they desired something. However, her babies were very well behaved for the most part and never really gave them any trouble outside of just being kids full of energy with a lively sense for adventure which she welcomed because she wanted them to explore and learn about the world they were growing up in. She wanted to teach them everything she knew and give them everything they needed to thrive in a world that was hard, but still one with so many opportunities to excel. Her husband lovingly referred to them as the inspiration behind the Hood Square Jr. clothing line which was for young kids. She absolutely admired her husband's drive to incorporate all aspects of his family life through their brand which is why she fully embraced her role as his Lady Hood Square.

She went to check on the kids to make sure that they had made their beds and to finish dressing them. The day's weather was suppose to be decent which meant that they only needed light jackets or sweaters to stay warm. They were taking the kids to Six Flags America which was located in the neighboring town of Bowie, Maryland. This would be their twelfth time going with the kids who loved it each and every time. It was a perk to have a large theme park literally a few miles away. It had always been close by for them to get to even when they stayed in their apartment in Uptown because everything in the DMV was within driving distance of each other. This could be said almost about the entire upper Eastern Seaboard because everything seemed so crowded and cramped out this way compared to the space of the Wild Wild West. Since living in DC, they had took a few trips up to the NYC to visit her grandparents and had driven twice as a way to sightsee because she loved a good old fashioned road trip where there was no rush to get to their destination. Nonetheless, a straight drive from where they lived in Prince George's County, Maryland to New York was only a three hour and thirty-seven minute drive.

"Mom that was fun," Khadija said being silly after getting off the Great Chase with her dad.

"Dija you was being a big scaredy-pants," Samir said mocking his sister.

"Mir you just mad I went on and you didn't. Who's the scaredy-pants now" Khadija replied to her brother poking her tongue at him.

"Y'all stop poking fun at each other and focus on having fun with each other," Sasha to her beautiful babies as they went exploring.

"Yeah, y'all make sure y'all listen to y'all mother," Kamal said while making funny faces at them that made everybody laugh.

"That's why your daughter so silly because her dad such a goofball," Sasha said lovingly as she touched her husband on the arm because she just couldn't resist any opportunity to have physical contact with him. A lot of it had to do with having to endure five long years of having to wait for him to come home to her, so even after having him home for over six years now, she found herself never getting tired of touching on him because even the simplest of contact sent a spark throughout her entire body.

"And you love this goofball," Kamal said lovingly as he leaned in for a peak on her luscious lips while getting lost in her pretty cat eyes that always held him captive in their gaze. He loved her so much and could never feel like he paid his debt to her that he owed her for holding him down while he was away. She was his purpose to continue doing what he did to do his part to improve life for them and make sure their kids didn't know any of the struggles they had to go through growing up.

"Y'all are so gross," Khadija said watching her parents' brief moment of passion that sent waves of energy out into the atmosphere which made her little brother bobbed his head to show he thought the same.

"Gross? I'm going to show y'all gross," Kamal said as he scoped up both of his big rug rats before they could escape and immediately started kissing both of them all over their cheeks and forehead.

Moments like this made all of the blood, sweat, and tears they had to have put in to be able to elevate and do more for their little family worth it, and if they had to do it again, they would add double the amount of each to recreate each and every single moment. Sasha was so in love with her husband and kids. Now a mother herself, she could fully understand and appreciate the fierceness of the love her own mother had given her and her brother all of their lives which continued into their adulthood.

By the time they left Six Flags America, the kids were fast asleep in the car seats she had for them in the backseats of her Kia Sorento which she loved because of the space a SUV offered. It was for sure a family car that was fit for small kids which is why she knew her thoughtful husband bought it in the first place. They had four cars in total now which included her 2021 green Nissan Maxima, her husband's 2020 all black Chevrolet Trailblazer, and 2020 black and lime green Dodge Charger SRT Hellcat Widebody which she occasionally bullied him out of when she wanted to feel the horsepower.

# CHAPTER THIRTY-THREE

## 2023

Tha Hood Square Movement nonprofit had received a boost in support after Kamal's sit down with the mayor of DC and the chief of the DC Metropolitan Police Department last month in December. The mayor had pledged her support and kept her promise of providing additional funding to help increase Hood Square's involvements with the inner-city youth of DC. Now Kamal along with all six of his DC mentors, almost a dozen of his part-time volunteer mentors, and about thirty of his Junior Hood Squares had been invited to the Washington Hilton in Northwest DC. The mayor was honoring Kamal with the Key to the City in recognition of his organization's outreach efforts to uplift the impoverished communities of DC. This was an honor of the highest regard because it symbolized the freedom of the recipient to enter and leave the city at will, as a trusted friend of the city residents.

Nevertheless, before the ceremony officially started at seven o'clock, a formal dinner was going to be held to raise money to help out the families of their Junior Hood Squares because all of the kids in their program came from very low-income families. Kamal sadly saw that more than half of the kids came from single parent homes and there were quite a few kids who were homeless. These kids had been living in the rough for so long that it was hard for some of them to open up enough to accept any kind of aid, but it was their mission as mentors to go after the most at risk of youth and try to save them from either a long life of incarceration or a short one to the grave.

Tha Hood Square Movement was also finally expanding into Maryland where its new and improved headquarters was set to open in Bowie by the end of March. They were partnering up with Bowie State University on increasing the outreach efforts into both Prince George's County and Charles County to the south. The objective was to start getting more of these hardened teens to stay in school, so they could graduate. Tha Hood Square Movement was going to be offering up Hood Square scholarships to the Junior Hood Squares that qualify to be able to attend Bowie State University upon successfully graduating high school. The scholarships were going to be offered to the ones most serious about wanting to further their education. These Junior Hood Squares were going to become eligible to participate in one of Bowie State University's many vocational training programs, their two-year associate program, or their full four-year undergraduate program. Kamal was very excited about being able to give these teens the opportunity to exceed expectations and really excel in life. He lived his life being an example that a person from a tough urban environment could refuse to let the limitations of the streets define them and instead decide to exceed expectations to become both Streetwise and Booksmart.

Nonetheless, the good news about this expansion was the fact that his DC Junior Hood Squares were also eligible to be awarded a Hood Square scholarship to attend Bowie State University because of the added support from the Mayor's Office of Community Affairs - Washington, DC and other donors who were really interested in seeing change bought to the less fortunate around DC Metropolitan area and beyond. This was a big part of the reason why tonight's ceremony was so important to the future of Tha Hood Square Movement in the DMV because DC was always considered to be its pulse. The more successes they had in DC consequently increased their potential for success into expanding into the areas that surrounded it, which ultimately led to the move to Maryland. Once they solidified their presence there, he planned to start reaching into Virginia as well.

"Baby, Sandy should be here soon," Sasha said stepping out the bathroom adjunct to their bedroom looking absolutely breathtaking in her royal blue gown and matching hijab. She had passed the Examination for Professional Practice in Psychology last year and was now a fully licensed psychologist in the Washington, DC Metropolitan area. She was getting ready to go through the steps to become board certified in Maryland as well.

"Yes I know Dr. Bukhari because she texted me the same message that she was on her way," Kamal replied getting lost in the beauty of his wife.

"Aww I will never get use to people calling me that even you Hubby. Baby why are you looking at me like that?" Sasha said coy like she had no idea why she had her husband staring with his jaw dropped.

"If the kids were asleep and our babysitter wasn't literally up the street, I would show why I'm staring at you like this," Kamal said looking her in her pretty eyes as he fixed up the cuff links on the black and gray three-piece suit he had on with the customized Hood Square tie.

"Oh really you would huh? Perhaps later tonight we will come back to this discussion, so I can find out what exactly you have in mind," Sasha said with a smile as she grabbed her purse and jacket that matched her outfit.

"You know I got you. My beautiful Honey Gurl," Kamal said as he went to gently embrace his wife and briefly kiss her, so not to crinkle her dress or mess up her makeup which she didn't really need at all because she was a natural beauty who could step out in buggy old sweats to go the store and still turn every head.

"You look so handsome husband," Sasha said admiring how he looked in his outfit with the dark gray kufi he had on his head that matched the tie and vest of his suit.

They left ten minutes later after Sandy had pulled up to watch the kids for the rest of the day until they got back home around midnight. The formal dinner was set to start around five o'clock in the evening which gave them about an hour to get to their destination. They were going to meet up with his mom, her parents, Jonny, and Trevor at the hotel because they all had flown out to DC in the past week to not miss this huge milestone for him and Tha Hood Square Movement.

They had decided to hop in his Hellcat Widebody since he barely drove it nowadays and took off for the open road. He loved the power of this car which made him feel like he was flying a jet plane every time he was behind the wheel. He had fell in love with Dodge Chargers every since driving the one his wife had had back when he was fresh out of prison. The model had proven to be a lifesaver literally when an old nemesis of his had tried to gun him down while he was on his way back to his mother's house where he had been staying at the time. This incident still plagued his mind because the coward had almost took him from his family. Nonetheless, it had been his need to be there for his family that made him leave Phoenix and come to DC where his wife who had been pregnant with their daughter Khadija was waiting instead of seeking revenge.

"Ladies and Gentlemen, I present the Key to the City to a dear friend of DC who has really made an impact since moving here and calling it a place of his own. Without further ado, I award this cere-monial key to you, Kamal Bukhari who we all know as Knerdie B aka Tha Real Hood Square," the mayor of DC said as she stepped to the side of the podium while handing him the box with the key inside.

As a result, Kamal took a brief moment to look at this pres-tigious award that he would have never of imagined he would be receiving especially in a place where he wasn't a native. The city of Washington, DC had long welcomed him with open arms and he would always consider it a home away from home. It held a very special place in his heart and he would forever be thankful for all their love and support.

"Man, man, what an honor to say in the least," Kamal said which made the crowd laugh a little bit, "Okay, since moving to DC back in 2017, I've seen nothing but love from you all. I've never thought while in prison that I would one day be standing in front of a crowd of supporters as the honoree for something I've developed growing up back in my hometown. Growing up in the inner-city which we fondly know as the hood, I was taught from an early age by my now deceased father a set of values that has given me the tools needed to succeed against all odds. These set of values are the foundation I built Hood Square upon and led me down the path to want to pass them on to the next generation which is why I started Tha Hood Square Movement in the first place as my attempt to address issues plaguing our neighborhoods. Lets say this, when I first came out here, I immediately fell in love with the culture of Chocolate City and was amazed that Hood Squares could be found out this way as well. Therefore, I knew that my mission was highly needed in DC. I followed my heart which is my beautiful wife Sasha and took a chance and made the move out here permanent by becoming a resident of this amazing city with so much black history tied to it. I love DC because it played a major part in molding me into the man standing humbly in front you all today. I can't express the gratitude I'm feeling for all the citizens up to our gracious mayor who has really been the spark behind the scenes that lit the fire that has made the movement rapidly spread further into the city and beyond. I thank you Ms. Mayor for the honor of being called friend to the city and I will make sure to continue onward with my outreach efforts to uplift our less fortunate and show our next generation that anybody and I mean anybody no matter on the block in the hood or locked in a cellblock, you, and I mean you, can improve your station in life to exceed expectations to become both Streetwise and Booksmart."

# CHAPTER THIRTY-FOUR

It had been a while since they had last came back to their hometown for a visit. This was their first trip back to Phoenix, Arizona for 2023. They arrived at Sky Harbor International Airport around eleven o'clock in the morning. The flight had taken almost five hours to get there nonstop. The kids who seemed to not feel any jet lag at all were excited because they were going to see their grandparents, uncles, aunts, and cousins. Sasha was happy too because she missed being around all their loved ones. They had gotten two rental cars for both of them to get around town during the this week-long trip. March was still fresh and spring had yet to come into season, but the legendary Arizona heat was already in full effect which quickly reminded them that they were back in the Valley of the Sun. They had been living on the East Coast for so long that they had lost their desert skin.

Nonetheless, it wasn't nothing like the feel of being home-sweet-home because for both herself and her husband, the Valley especially the South Side would forever be where their roots were planted. They had booked a room at the Pointe South Mountain Resort located in South Phoenix to be close to all their relatives who stayed throughout South Phoenix, Ahwatukee, and Chandler. The kids took off running as soon as they saw their welcoming party which consisted of her parents, her mother-in-law, her big brother with his wife and their eldest child, and her aunt.

"Hey everybody, mamí, papí, Mama Salma, bro, sis, tia, and my handsome nephew," Sasha said as they walked towards their loved ones who were all vying for the attention of Khadija and Samir.

"Sassy, oh niece I've missed you," Marie said emotionally while hugging her tight after rushing to meet her.

"Aww, I've missed you too tia," Sasha replied emotionally as well.

"Marie, let my baby girl go so I could get my hugs," Sammy said as he walked up to his daughter and son-in-law who was having an emotional moment with his mother.

"Okay, okay, but you know girl we gotta catch up during this week. Me, yo moms, and Karen already got a day planned just for us girls. Yes, that includes you, little cutie," Marie said pinching her great niece Khadija on her cheek and hugging her tight for a second.

"Yes we do hija. Come here so mamí can get all the love and affection," Sabrina said as she got in her hugs with her daughter. "Bestie, girl you looking like you ready to pop any day now," Sasha said as she gently touched her sister-in-law's protruding belly.

"Nicca, I can't wait to give birth to this one cuz she has already been a handful inside. She stay kicking. Keep yo hand there cuz she may start up again," Karen said which made her husband Tru smile as he too hugged his sister.

"Aww, my little niece I can't wait to meet you, but where are my other little nieces?" Sasha said as she went back to her sister-in-law's belly for a second time.

"They are with my parents who can't wait for y'all to pull up," Karen replied.

"As Salamu Alaikum Mama Salma," Sasha said greeting and hugging her mother-in-law.

"Wa Alaikum as Salam. I'm so happy to see you and Mali back because it's been too long since I got to see y'all and my grand babies in the flesh," Salma said.

"I know, I know because that's what my mom been on us about also," Sasha said.

"I'm glad we finally were able to make it though because you're right mom, we don't get to spend quality time with y'all often enough," Kamal said who was catching up with his brother-in-law and father-in-law.

The kids went off to the side to have a little powwow with their big cousin Lil Santi. It touched her heart to watch them all interact with each other. They all got ready to leave now that they had their luggage and the car rentals were ready for them to pick up. The drive from the airport which was located in East Phoenix to her parents' house in South Phoenix didn't take that long at all. Her parents still stayed in her old neighborhood, Park South. She couldn't help but reminisce every time she came back to visit. However, a lot had changed over the years due to gentrification. The Roeser Apartments which had been a staple in her hood since she could remember had long since been knocked down and replaced with the Grandfamilies Place Apartments.

Nevertheless, this was the South Side, so some things never changed because no matter how much development they built around the hoods, it still didn't stop the violence from old rivalries that never died out. Once inside, she couldn't help but feel her heart warm at seeing her old room still put together like she had left it all them years ago when she had first moved to Washington, DC for college. Their kids were going to be spending their first two days staying with her parents before going to stay with their grandma Salma who still stayed in her old house located in the neighborhood known as Southern. Then they were going to spend one day with their great aunt before coming to stay the last few days at the hotel with their parents who planned to be on the flight back to DC that following Sunday night. This would allow the kids a chance to spend some quality time with their Arizona family while allowing Sasha and her husband to attend to some much-needed business matters. They would also get spend a little alone time with each other at the resort.

"Congratulations again baby girl because mi hija is finally a psychologist," Sammy said proudly in front of everybody.

"That's good because now she can treat yo crazy self," Sabrina said poking fun at her husband while also feeling proud to see her daughter making such major strides in her life.

"And I would gladly sit down with my baby and let her know just how crazy her mom is too," Sammy said laughing while winking at his daughter which made all the adults laugh because all the kids had wondered off to play videogames in her brother's old room.

"Sassy, now you can properly diagnose both of yo nutjobs for parents and finally see that yo tia is the only sane one around," Marie said jokingly.

"I would love to one day have my own private practice, but for now I'm using my expertise to help run Tha Hood Square Movement. I'm planning to implement a Lady Hood Square inspired program geared towards the empowerment of our young women of color throughout America," Sasha said proudly.

"Aww, that's what's up niece because they are so many young women who need to see a woman like you doing what you do to encourage them that they can do it too. You represent multiple things being black, Latina, Muslim, and now well into motherhood as a straight up boss bitch," Marie said with attitude because she couldn't help herself when she was also inspired by her niece who had come a long way from her days as Lady Fierce.

"You said that right," Karen said who was sitting comfortably in the recliner with her husband standing right next to her clearly at her beck-and-call.

"Girl, yes. My daughter then bossed all the way up," Sabrina said.

"Well, I learned how to be a boss from some bona fide boss ladies," Sasha said pausing to look at her mother, aunt, mother-in-law, and sister-in-law all individually in the eye before she continued, "And now I plan to use this knowledge to benefit all of the Lady Hood Squares out there. Bestie, I have to say that you have outdone yourself with the line which has allowed for Lady Hood Square to grow immensely in popularity, and is why the movement resonates with so many young women throughout this country no matter if they come from a hood or not."

"Listen to my Baby preach. You are the embodiment of Lady Hood Square mi amor which is why you are known as Lady Hood Square," Kamal said admiring his wife. They had recently went through a slew of interviews with popular podcasts and radio shows across the country to promote the new additions to their clothing lines while also getting the message of the movement out there to a bigger audience. Consequently, now he didn't know how they were going to find the time to do everything after the summer once they launched their own podcast called, *"Tha Real Hood Square Podcast"* and went touring around the country on speaking engagements because they had been booked well in advance. He never knew that they could make such a living off being motivational speakers. He was truly going to enjoy just showing up to speak his mind for thirty minutes up to an hour.

"Aww, husband you know that you inspire and push me always to do better. I love you so much and can't thank you enough for always supporting me," Sasha as she kissed him passionately in front of everybody not caring one bit.

They chilled for the better part of the afternoon with their loved ones before they had to go check into their hotel room. Now alone, they took the opportunity to get real cozy with each other because tomorrow was going to be a hectic day meeting up with Jonny and the West Coast team about the future of the brand. Jonny was proposing that they consider moving the headquarters out of Arizona to be a bigger market like LA or the NYC, but her husband was totally against it because Arizona was forever to be the epicenter of Hood Square. He felt this way because as Tha Real Hood Square himself, it was Arizona, South Phoenix to be exact, where the brand and the movement were birthed. The Valley of the Sun and Gun had transformed him into Knerdie B. As the Co-CEO of Hood Square, she would be required to attend the board meeting and listen attentively to both sides before she gave her professional opinion one way or another.

# CHAPTER THIRTY-FIVE

He had his son with him as he prepared to head to the Islamic Community Center of Tempe for al Juma'ah services. Sasha had left hours ago with their daughter to go have their girls only spa day, so that left just them to go have a guys only day. They were going to meet up with his O' G homies Trevor and Ahmad at the mosque before going to Ahwatukee where his Boyz still stayed with their sons and wives. Consequently, the past week back in the Valley had been filled with a lot of catching up and reminiscing with loved ones he haven't been physical around in a long while.

They had let the kids spend their first few days staying with their grandparents and their great aunt. The kids had had a great time of being spoiled with gift after gift. Nevertheless, Kamal and Sasha had used that time to deal with their responsibilities of overseeing both Hood Square and Tha Hood Square Movement while they were in the desert. As a result, he was very pleased to see what he knew already from the reports he got daily that the operations for both his clothing lines and the Arizona branch of his nonprofit were running smoothly. He had promoted Trevor to the position of Chief Operating Officer of Tha Hood Square Movement which made him second in rank only to Kamal and Sasha's roles as Co-Executive Directors. This resulted in Trevor being responsible for the entire West Coast. He was already about spread the movement into Las Vegas, Nevada and Denver, Colorado where the brand had a very strong following.

Kamal had also finally got to see the new base of operations for Tha Hood Square Movement in the Valley where Trevor's office was located as well as the mentors and staff who worked for him.

This included the highly decorated former Phoenix gang taskforce detective, Sam Williams who was the co-creator of the their highly successful gang diversion program called ReSet. Trevor had decided to move from the Hood Square headquarters located in Tempe four months ago to a location in South Phoenix to further separate the growing nonprofit arm from the for-profit arm of Hood Square. This insured that each arm could now exclusively focus more on their individual missions.

Nonetheless, the highlight of being around the Arizona movement was to get to meet all the new Junior Hood Squares which included some of his little homies from the Front Street Boyz. His old squad was still very popular with the youngsters coming out of his hood and had taken a life of its own since the days of the original four members. Kamal still to this day missed his ace homie S Dogg who had been slain when they were teens. He was glad that him and his Boyz had kept their brotherly bond tight throughout these years. They had swore to always be their brother's keeper. This vow extended to S Dogg's little brother because Lil S Dogg had always been like a little brother to them.

The Valley had turned up once word had gotten out that Tha Real Hood Square and Lady Hood Square were back in town. They had been getting invites from all over which really touched them, but they simply didn't have the time to fit anything else in without sacrificing the little family time they were being afforded in their week-long trip because the trip was both business and pleasure. This is why the last few days were going to be exclusively for spending quality time with their loved ones they barely saw nowadays.

"Ahki, it has been a blessing to see you continuing to grow and develop," Ahmad said after they were leaving the mosque to go eat lunch with each other before Kamal left to go visit his Boyz.

"The same can be said about you O' G because I'm so happy to see you and Trevor both doing so good after walking off all that time," Kamal replied.

"Al hamdu Allah, we all are free from Tha System that tried so hard to break us. However, we came out of that forge harder than steel instead," Trevor said as they walked the short distance to the Phoenicia Café.

"You got that right O' G. Oh yeah, I've been loving what I've been seeing about the Hood Square videogame your son is developing for us," Kamal said.

"Yeah, Baby Tre don't play when it comes to his profession or let me say professions because my boy a game designer and a bona fide professional gamer who is getting paid some pretty big money to sit down and do what we did as kids for free," Trevor said.

"Yeah, he is one of the top e-athletes in the nation for real. The way my son already loves his games, I wouldn't be surprised if he grew up to be just like Baby Tre in'sha Allah," Kamal.

"And your lil mans is such a young handsome fella," Ahmad said as he gave Samir a fist bump.

"He gets his good looks from his mama," Kamal said with a smile truly enjoying being in such good company. These were two of the main people who had been behind the reason he had come out of prison so strong and motivated to hit the ground running and never look back. He had been talking with both of them about potentially expanding the reach of Tha Hood Square Movement into the very system they all had been trapped in. Ahmad had suggested possibly going back in as a volunteer mentor and representative of Hood Square to start their outreach to the formerly incarcerated before they got release. This was such a good idea that Kamal immediately gave his full approval for Trevor to start reaching out to their contacts at Central Office which was the headquarters for the Arizona Department of Corrections Rehabilitation and Reentry.

After lunch, Kamal made the short drive to get to where his Boyz lived. He was excited to come hang out with them because since being back, he hadn't had the opportunity to pull up till now. Nonetheless, they had met up with him twice during the week for quick encounters while he was at the his office at the Hood Square headquarters.

"What's brackin' with my bro?" Brazy said as they came out to greet him.

"Fasho, dam Swan, it's sure feels good to welcome you back to our humble abodes," Outlaw said as they were embracing each other.

"There is nothing humble about y'all mini mansions," Kamal said laughing because his Boyz lived in some pretty nice homes that they had really hooked up throughout the years they been living in them.

"Look at my lil nephew looking like his mama thankfully," Brazy said which made them all laugh.

"The same can be said about my nephews as well," Kamal said looking at their sons who were both now eleven years old.

"We all don't have any problems with that because we all got some real fine dimes for wives," Outlaw said which was the truth because Sasha, Ms. Chel'le, and Twennie were without a doubt breathtakingly beautiful.

"Y'all niggas wanna head to my game room?" Brazy said since they were all at his house. Outlaw literally stayed a short walk down the block from him. The brothers had grown up super close and had maintained that closeness into adulthood which also could be seen in the brother-like relationship between their sons who were their juniors in everything.

It felt good to be hanging with his Boyz like the good old days when they were known as the squad of all squads on the South Side especially with having their sons experience the unbreakable bond they shared. The original squad were all fathers now handling their responsibilities to their families. In his opinion, Kamal felt that there was nothing more standup than a man handling his business and fulfilling his obligations to his wife and kids. This was one of the many lessons he had learned from his own father who had died before his thirteenth birthday.

"You still going to see the homie tomorrow?" Outlaw had asked while they were playing the newest installment of *Call Of Duty* online against players from all over the world.

"Yes, I had scheduled the visit last week in advance since that's the way they are doing contact visits," Kamal replied.

"Yeah we heard that from bro," Brazy said.

"Where my nigga at again?" Outlaw said.

"They got bro on this private yard called La Palma in Eloy. From what I've heard it looks nothing like any yard I've ever been to. Bro said he loved it over there because them niggas be out all day playing videogames and doing them," Kamal said.

"They need to hurry up and free my nigga Ticko Loon for real," Outlaw said.

"Fasho, free my nigga Ticko Loon the Goon," Brazy said passionately which made their sons look at him like he was crazy which he was which is how he got his hood name in the first place.

"Yeah they need to free our Gangsta, but as of right now bro ain't set to come home till 2029 in'sha Allah," Kamal said because Ticko Loon had been down already ten years on a sixteen year sentence which was flat time.

"We be hitting that nigga on the tablet fasho making sure he knows he is well missed," Outlaw said.

"We gotta do a song for him, so we can drop the video of us with Free The Goon shirts," Brazy said.

"That shit gone be hot fasho. We can shoot the video on the Way, so we can have our Gangstas in it," Outlaw said.

"Yeah I would make sure I come back to be a part of that. Y'all new song '*Southern Stupid*' slapping for real. I've been putting niggas on to y'all music in DC and I can say they loving that real desert flow," Kamal said.

They all hung out well into the night catching up and reminiscing about their From Boyz To Men days when S Dogg was still alive. Kamal's life as he knew had changed forever the moment he had saw his ace homie getting gunned down right in front of him.

He had almost gotten gunned down too if it wasn't for S Dogg saving his life by pushing him out of the way, but he had still succumbed injuries from being shot once in his shoulder and bumping his head really hard into the car he fell into. Nonetheless, that Dangerous Path he had went on had long since turned into a full blown Redemption story of triumph.

---

# CHAPTER THIRTY-SIX

The view from the rooftop of their little cave hotel seemed to be surreal, if not magical. For the past three days they had been on their week-long baecation for their tenth year wedding anniversary which was going to be their last full day on June eleventh. They had decided to come to the most charming little town called Greme located in the semi-arid region of Cappadocia in central Turkey. The town was famous for its unique rock formations and amazing hot air ballooning opportunities. Walking through town their first day had made Sasha feel like they had been transported into the majestic world of Aladdin. She was for sure feeling like Princess Jasmine with all the romantic jesters and pampering she was receiving from her husband. He was giving her the royal treatment and she couldn't get enough of it.

This morning, they had woken up early again to catch the beautiful sunrise with the hot air balloons as its backdrop. This had quickly become one of their favorite pastimes which made getting one of the famous cave hotels with a rooftop worth it. Today they were planning to visit the huge carpet shop called Sultan Carpets which was located in the center of town to browse for new rugs to add to their collection. They already owned a few authentic Turkish and Persian rugs that decorated their home, but these were going to be their first ones bought actually in the country of origin which gave them a whole new feel of authenticity. Sasha was excited because they had never been to any store remotely close to how elegant this one was which seemed timeless like it came from an era the world over had long since forgotten. This was their first time to this part of the world. Since his release, her husband had been wanting for them to take more international trips to Africa and the Middle East. They had already made plans to finally take a family trip with his mother-in-law to visit her home country of Mali located in West Africa in the beginning of next year.

Nonetheless, their most important trip they were planning to take to this part of world was set for 2025 when they planned to finally make hajj to Makkah located in the country of Saudi Arabia. It had been a desire of hers since becoming a Muslima all them years ago while her husband had been away. They were very devout Muslims who took their Islamic way of life serious, so fulfilling this Pillar of Islam was a top priority for the both of them. It was a once in a lifetime obligation for every adult Muslim who could afford it, to make hajj. The trip was going to include their kids, her mother-in-law and her husband, and a few of their closest friends who were Muslim.

"I love you like I love no other," Sasha said as she snuggled up closer to him on the makeshift hamlet they had put together on the rooftop to get extra cozy as they looked in the horizon.

"And I love you like I love no other," Kamal replied making sure to hold her tight and really enjoy the moment with the love of his life.

By mid morning, they found themselves getting lost in rows and rows of rugs. Consequently, with so many beautiful designs to choose from, they couldn't make up their minds on what to select. Her husband, however, had had his eye on one particular hand knotted wool-on-wool rug with a Turkish Oushak design they had passed by a few minutes ago, but had chosen to still browse before they made up their minds. They didn't have the shop all to themselves because there was other tourists from all over the world with the same intention on their minds as them walking around mesmerized by all the beautiful rugs that came in all kinds of sizes and colors.

"I know you want to get some new prayer rugs also, but I will never bow my head on another while at home when I have the one you gave me all them years ago before you came home," Sasha said holding his hand tight.

"Aww, I know Wifey that it holds a special place in your heart and will forever be your rug of choice. It still touches my heart to pray with you and see you stepping on it," Kamal said looking at her and getting lost as usual in her pretty hazel eyes.

"I want us to try flying in one of the hot air balloons before we leave, so we can get a bird's eye view of this beautiful place in'sha Allah," Sasha said seriously.

"Baby, are you sure?" Kamal said looking at her because she was notoriously scared of heights which made her never take the window seat when they flew.

"Yes, I am sure because this is a once in a lifetime opportunity to get a feel of what Aladdin and Princess Jasmine may have felt riding on their magic carpet above town," Sasha said with the most beautiful smile.

"Okay my Love, we will schedule it for Friday morning in'sha Allah," Kamal said kissing her on the cheek.

Towards the end of the day, they went to the Red Valley to go on a hike. They were amazed to see the sharp sandstone ridges glow a deep, vibrant red as the sun burned into the unique landscape in the last moments of sunset. They quickly pulled out the traveler's prayer rugs they had brought with them for this trips and got ready to make the Sunset Prayer together. This trip was what they had been needing to really get a break from all the busybody activities of home because they would never had found themselves outdoors going on a hike just to catch a spectacular view of the sun as it set. This trip was going to go down as one of the best they had ever taken. Sasha felt so at peace and would recommend that they take this trip again for their fifteenth year wedding anniversary and make it their destination after every five years of marriage afterwards. She got into position beside her husband, her lover, her everything and got ready to make prayer feeling the perfection of this moment locked itself in her memory banks...

# EPILOGUE

The second season of the youth summer league had officially started July eighth. They were now two weeks in on a six week schedule and things couldn't have been going any better. In fact, things were going way better than Kamal could have ever imagined with the big sponsors they had received in the last few months which gave them access to resources to rapidly expand the original six teams from last year to now ten teams representing different parts of Washington, DC. He knew the boost in support had been a direct result from being a recipient of the most prestigious Key to the City. As a result, Tha Hood Square Ballers which was now the official name of the DC Metro youth summer basketball league had gained the attention of celebrities like players from the Washington Wizards who had come on as volunteer coaches and mentors to help run the expansion.

Tha Hood Square Movement was now operating in Maryland where its new DMV headquarters was based in Bowie. He was making big moves to bring it to Baltimore with the help of one of his old cellies and mentors, Askari who had finally been released after doing almost forty years in prison. Askari was a Baltimore native and legend in both the streets and the prison system. The Maryland Department of Corrections had shipped him out to the Arizona Department of Corrections years ago as way to muzzle him, but the move had only made his bark louder and prouder. Kamal had been thrilled when he had first gotten word from his O' G homie that he was out and back in his backyard where he wanted to see the outreach mentorship program come make a difference for the youth and formerly incarcerated.

The future of Hood Square and Tha Hood Square Movement was looking brighter than ever. The brand had come a long ways since the days of its conception when he had first started designing it in a max custody prison cell. Now he had a team of people which included his wife, the Lady Hood Square who were more intelligent and creative than he could ever be taking it to new levels he didn't know existed. They had long proven the motto to be true because they weren't never going away. He was so happy to see what had originated in his mind well on its way to becoming a household name. Hood Square: it's not a moment, it's a Movement!